Vanessa Lafaye was born in Florida and studied in North Carolina. She moved to the UK in 1999 (having been deported once) and is the author of two novels, *Summertime* and *At First Light*. Her debut *Summertime* was chosen for the Richard and Judy Book Club in 2015 and was shortlisted for the Historical Writers Award. Vanessa passed away in February 2018.

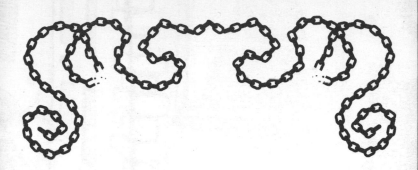

Miss Marley

A seasonal tale of kindness and goodwill

Vanessa Lafaye
with Rebecca Mascull

ONE PLACE. MANY STORIES

HQ
An imprint of HarperCollins*Publishers* Ltd
1 London Bridge Street
London SE1 9GF

This hardback edition 2018

1

First published in Great Britain by
HQ, an imprint of HarperCollins*Publishers* Ltd 2018

Author's Note

This story is one of pure invention. I have long been fascinated by Dickens' *A Christmas Carol*, finding new meaning and new dimensions with every version that I have studied. However, the one character who intrigued me the most, the one on whom the whole tale seems to hang, appears in only three brief scenes: Jacob Marley.

Doomed to drag his chains across the earth for all eternity, yet determined to help Scrooge avoid his fate, Marley seems to me an extremely complex character. I wondered what Marley had done to deserve his desperately severe punishment. Surely, I thought, it would take more than what he quotes to Scrooge – the fact that he neglected his fellow man and never left the counting house?

Since Dickens chose to deny us any more insight into this enigmatic figure, I started to wonder about Marley's life story, an exercise which gradually consumed my imagination. I wanted to understand the events which shaped him, which led him to be the man he is as Scrooge's partner – and then to regret this so bitterly that he returns from the grave to put things right.

I have invented a sister, Clara Belle Marley, to give us the answers to these questions. I confess that the idea of inhabiting Marley himself felt too much like trespassing. Through the eyes of Clara, a character purely of my own creation, I can tell my invented story freely.

That said, I was so conscious of the love and reverence felt for the original, that it was almost impossible not to be paralysed by self-consciousness as I wrote this. I hope that other devotees of *A Christmas Carol*, and Dickens' work in general, will grant me license to explore Marley and his unseen, yet pivotal, role in this classic tale.

Vanessa Lafaye, February 2018

Contents

PART I: THE BEGINNING

Chapter 1

Clara Belle Marley jostled among the other children for a spot in front of Mr Quoit's toy shop window. The small boy with the crutch was the only one to whom she gave quarter. The rest got sharp elbows and a hard stare. Her ankles were sunk in melting snow, and she had wet snowflakes on her shoulders, but she did not care. For a few spare moments, this was her place of escape.

Her eyes swept over the painted boats, the toy soldiers, the porcelain-faced dolls with their unblinking stares, the rocking horse with real leather reins, the spinners and hooters and trumpets. For pride of place was taken by a doll's house. But not just any doll's house. With its blue slate roof, white rendered walls, and red front door, it was the image in miniature of all they had lost. Hampstead House had been a happy, comfortable home, which the doll's house replicated in every detail. The furnishings were sumptuous, just as Mama loved, with swagged and tasselled curtains, and colourful rugs on the floor. It caused her special pain to see the figures of two adults, plus a boy and girl child, seated at a wooden table with a tiny, delicate tea set. It was at this time of the afternoon that they always took tea, served by Dorothy.

That was before.

She forced herself to study every detail, not to look away even when the sadness threatened to overwhelm her, all the while surrounded by the excited gabbling of the other children. The golden light spilling from the window gave their upturned faces a glow, smoothing away pallor, dirt, and bruises. Several were street children like her and Jake, but some still had families, judging from the scarves tightly wound around little necks, and carefully mended jackets.

More than anything, Clara wanted to be part of a family again.

Jake pushed his way through the crowd to her side to pull roughly at her sleeve. 'Come on, Clara! There'll be none left if we don't hurry!'

Every Friday afternoon, the butcher threw scraps from his back door to the hungry street children, but all the best morsels went to bigger boys and vicious stray dogs.

Clara reminded herself again, as the snow sloshed

into her thin shoes, of the before time. There had been spiced punch and sugared chestnuts, roast turkey and gravy, berry-studded garlands sparkling with baubles, and Mother and Father beaming as they opened their presents. Every window blazed with light and warmth. She muttered the words under her breath like a rosary.

It wasn't always like this.

In the butcher's yard, a bigger boy, a map of scars across his face, pushed her to the ground, but Jake was there. With one punch, the other boy went down and Jake howled in triumph, prize clutched in his fist: a pig's trotter, only partially gnawed by a dog. She recognised the other boy from the workhouse but didn't know his name. The workhouse, so dreaded before they passed through its huge iron gates, seemed like a dream now.

'Let's go.' Jake steered her away from the growling dogs. 'There's nothing left worth fighting for here.'

She blew on her frozen fingers.

Indeed, between the children and the dogs, the butcher's yard was spotless. The man himself stood in a rectangle of golden light at the back door in his bloodied apron on this dark winter's afternoon, sharpening a cleaver, watching the drama unfold but never interfering. His wife had more of a kind spirit. Sometimes she ladled out some leftover broth, when her husband wasn't there to see, the steam sticking her coarse grey curls to her face.

Around the corner of the next alley, in their special spot behind the draper's, they stopped to survey their haul. In addition to the pig's foot, they had some turnip tops, a half-rotten potato, and some cabbage leaves with only a little mould. Jake dumped it all into their pot – just a metal tin with no handle – and went in search of water. Among the ordure of the alley, Clara shuffled for paper and sticks to make a fire, already imagining its warmth in her bony fingers. She pulled the shreds of her shawl tighter around her shoulders and stamped her numb feet.

Jake returned just as the twigs caught the flame. He held the pot above the fire until it started to bubble, scratching his lice bites with the other hand, his eyes alight with hunger that she knew was mirrored in her own. Hunger was their constant companion, sharing every moment of every day, like one of the mange-ridden dogs which shadowed their steps. It was there to greet them at sunrise, there all during the long day as they searched for food, until they curled up together against the cold, damp wall in their corner, stomachs growling with emptiness. In the fire's glow, Jake's face, once so smooth and boyish, was all sharp angles and harsh lines. And this at only twelve years old.

The smell of pork and vegetables tickled her nose and she became fearful, lest someone be attracted to the odour and steal their hard-won meal. There were other street children to be wary of, sometimes more dangerous than adults. They would snatch even the smallest morsel from between one's teeth, or yank the bread from your fingers. So she and Jake huddled together over the pot, shoving the food into their mouths as fast as the heat allowed. A shuffling sound alerted her to the presence of Martha, one of the Crawlers. They were no threat. Too weak even to beg, too weak to do anything more than crawl along the ground, they were the lowest of the low. Martha acknowledged Clara with a nod, and crawled off into the shadows.

Food safely in their bellies, she leaned against Jake, where he rested against the crusty wall. His arm went around her shoulders and he kissed the top of her head.

'A plum pudding now, I reckon,' he said, already drifting off to sleep. The fire's glow warmed her feet. It would soon go out, and they would have only each other for warmth through the long night. Fire attracted attention, which was never welcome.

'Mother's plum pudding,' she said, mouth watering again at the memory of crystallised fruits, steamed puddings and custard – a huge jug of which only the beefy arms of the cook, Dorothy, could handle. And then she was back there again, in the tall white house on Hampstead Street. It seemed to be as far away as India, not just across the Thames from them, but it might as well have been on the moon; the heartless moon whose cold, silver light trickled down between the rooftops. A clear night, with no cloud, would be a cold night. She snuggled in closer to Jake, his bony ribs against hers.

'And Father will make a toast and light the brandy,' he said, 'and we will sing, God Rest Ye—'

Clara took up the tune in her high, breathy voice, 'Let nothing you dismay.' But then a coughing fit took her, which ended with tears.

'Clara Belle,' Jake pulled her closer. 'Don't cry, my Clara Belle. Tomorrow will be better.' It was what he said every night. 'We'll find a way to get you some medicine.'

'But how? With no money?' The coughing wracked her until she was limp.

'I will find a way,' he said.

'Make me the promise,' she sniffed.

And so he said the words he had said every night for the past nine months, since they were forced to leave Hampstead Street for the workhouse. 'I promise that we will have a good life again. And I will always keep you safe. And those who have wronged us will live to regret it.' This last was an addition to the promise, and she turned her face up to his.

'Uncle Robert?'

Jake nodded. 'And others.'

She shivered as she recalled the day, the wretched day, when Uncle Robert visited them in Hampstead Street, the house all decked in black crepe. He had always seemed so amiable, but now he eyed up the furnishings, and Mother and Father's treasured possessions, with the critical look of a professional auctioneer.

'Of course, you understand,' he had said, in a much more businesslike tone than she remembered, 'you cannot remain here. Tragic as it is to lose both parents, you are still too young and, unfortunately, my brother's only legacy to you is his debts.'

Dorothy hovered in the doorway, red-nosed from crying, twisting a dishcloth. 'I could look after 'em here, Master Marley. They're like my own—'

'Impossible,' pronounced Uncle Robert. 'As I said, my brother has not left the means to sustain this,' and here his eyes roved over Mother's pale blue silk curtains with the silver tassels, 'lifestyle. This house must be sold to recoup some of the shortfall.'

'Well, where shall the mites go to live, beggin' your pardon, sir? And who shall look after them?'

Here Uncle Robert narrowed his eyes. 'Dorothy, I was expecting some tea.'

'Right away, Master Marley.' Dorothy scuttled back to the kitchen, wiping her eyes with the dishcloth.

Uncle Robert stroked the damask upholstery which matched the curtains. Clara had been with Mama when she chose it, just after they moved in. The same colour as her eyes, the clear, liquid blue of a winter sky. She recalled Mother's delight at the way the material danced in the sunlight which poured through the large bay window.

That was only six months before the pox took her. Six months of undiluted joy was what Clara had to remember, what she clung to now, in the freezing filth of the alley.

After Mother's death, things changed with the dizzying speed of a carnival ride. The Inspector of Nuisances arrived the next day to inform them that the pox rendered their house uninhabitable until it had been cleansed top to bottom with sulphur, along with all their possessions. The public disinfectors would arrive in the morning, he said, and the Marleys would need to vacate the premises until they had completed their task.

Red-eyed with shock and grief, Father had simply nodded and said, 'Of course. Of course, at once.'

Uncle Robert had been so kind then, taking them all in to his more modest house, sitting up late every night with Father. They all simply existed in a frozen cocoon of grief. Father's answer to everything, without question or reflection, was, 'Of course, at once.' So when Uncle Robert proposed some business investments, as a way for Father to get back on his feet, his reply was the same.

Clara did not understand the nature of these investments, but it wasn't long before loud arguments could be heard between Father and Uncle Robert, emanating from behind Robert's study door.

They were back living in the sulphurous house on Hampden Street, minus many of the furnishings which Uncle Robert had kindly sold for them, when a police constable arrived one day, asking for Father. Dorothy explained that he was at work, but the constable informed them that he had not been at his place of business for almost a month. It appeared that the constable's duty was to take Father to the Coldbath Fields Prison, where he was to be incarcerated as a debtor.

The constable returned later that day, demeanour entirely changed, clenching his cap in his hands.

When Dorothy answered the door, he said, 'I'm very sorry to tell you that we have located a ... person whom we believe to be Mr Edmund Marley.' And he produced Father's top hat, stained with river mud. Dorothy fainted right there on the brass doorstep that she polished every day.

It seemed that he had drowned somewhere near Putney Bridge. Some mudlarks, out early to meet the low tide, had found him. What made Clara cry longest and hardest was the image of him, flailing in the foamy brown water, still wearing that hat. He was never without that hat. She had to think of him falling, not jumping. The inquest, perhaps out of kindness to his two white-faced orphans, returned an open verdict.

She sniffled again now, and felt Jake stroke her hair. She sought the comfort of the dream, as she did every night. In her old bed, in the room with the white lilac wallpaper, Mother is sitting beside her on the counterpane, stroking her hair, humming a tuneless lullaby. The pillow is soft under her head, a copper bed-warmer toasty on the sheet by her feet. She is content. Safe and content.

A commotion around a bend in the alley shattered her into wakefulness. Jake was already on his feet, running towards the direction of the sound, blade in hand.

When she caught up to him, panting and blurry

with sleep, Jake was standing over the man slumped against the wall. The red of the blood splashing onto the white cravat at his neck matched his garnet waistcoat and britches. In the flickering lamplight from the street, he reached out a hand. 'Help me,' he gurgled.

Hand to her throat, she exclaimed in horror, 'Jake, what did you do?'

'Quiet. I did nothing, I found him like this. Those who done it are gone, I saw them scarper, that way.' His blade was clean but his eyes were wild.

She knelt beside the man, whose plump cheeks were already losing their ruddy sheen. Blood pumped steadily from the wound in his neck. There had been a series of garrottings in the neighbourhood. A special police squad had even been formed to try to deal with them.

'Help me,' the man repeated, a bloodied hand on her arm. His eyes, unseeing, swept her face.

'We need to sound the alarm!' she said. There was so much blood, but not enough light to see where it was coming from. It pooled at her feet, glossy black.

Jake knelt beside her and shook the man's shoulder. 'What'll you give us?'

'They took—' gasped the man. 'They took my purse. Please, I—'

Pity vied with disgust in Clara's mind. He was as fat

13

as a Christmas turkey, his bulging waistcoat stained with gravy and port. His rattling breath was rich with it. He was obviously on his way home after a fine dinner when he was attacked. The taste of pig's foot and rotten vegetables rose in her throat.

'You have another one, don't cha?' said Jake. 'Quick now, give it to me, and help is on the way. Come on, not much time left.'

The man scrabbled vaguely at his crotch. Clara scuttled backwards, but Jake undid the man's belt and fished around in his underclothes until his hand emerged clutching a purse. Butter-yellow leather, it bulged with coins which clinked softly.

'Ha!' Jake kept his voice low, eyes flitting in all directions. 'I knew it. Let's go.' And he pulled Clara roughly to her feet.

'But what about—?'

'Nothing to be done for him' Jake said, with a wave of his hand. 'He is a goner. And besides,' he said, as he pulled her along, 'he'd have stepped over our dead bodies to get to his carriage.'

The man made a gurgling sound, and Clara turned her back.

So began their new life.

Chapter 2

Their first room was hardly more than a cupboard. It smelled of damp, and the winter gales sent icy fingers to rattle the window frame, but there was a small coal fire and a bed. Clara had her first wash in nine months from the cracked jug on its stand in the corner, and felt like a princess.

The landlady, a Scot called Mrs Clayburn, clearly had grave reservations about even allowing them over the threshold, but when Jake held out a palm full of coins, she had a change of heart, muttering, 'I'm a martyr to my charitable nature.' She reminded Clara of a pigeon; totally grey, from her unwashed bonnet to her puffy bosom and down to her dingy slippers, glittering black eyes like shards of flint.

After a room and a wash, their next mission was a meal. They found a pub nearby, the Ox and Plough, where they made a similar impression on the landlord. Only when Jake produced more coins were they allowed entry. There they had stringy beef and vegetables boiled to mush and they mopped every drop of gravy from the plates with hunks of stale bread, washed down with mugs of bitter ale. The other diners, huddled over their food in the smoky gloom, paid them no mind at all.

Tucked up in bed that night, stomach complaining at the unaccustomed bounty instead of cramped with emptiness, Clara didn't notice the coarseness of the sheets or the suspicious stains on the pillows, or feel the rough floorboards against her feet. They had a home again, a roof and four walls. With an address, they could get work.

'Tomorrow will be better,' murmured Jake with a satisfied belch, teetering on the edge of sleep.

Clara tried to stifle the cough, so as not to disturb him, but it overcame her in waves that left her gasping.

He held her close. 'And we shall get you something for that.'

In the morning, after a breakfast of tea with milk, and bread with butter (butter!), they joined the thronging streets. The crisp winter air smelled of roasting chestnuts, horse manure, coal smoke and holly. The sharp scent of pine rose from the bowers that decked every corner. Blurred sunlight was making some headway against the choking fog which had lain across the city for days. A biting wind blew a few wisps of snow which caught in Clara's eyelashes. She pulled the shawl tighter around her neck.

Jake shouldered his way through the hawkers and vendors, the coffee merchants and flower-sellers, the boot-blacks and card tricksters to the street doctor with his tray of wares.

They waited for an old woman to leave with her paper parcel, then Jake asked, 'How much for the cough drops?'

The street doctor eyed him and Clara with interest. 'Depends on what type of cough you got: dry or wet, chesty or wheezy, bloody or not.'

At that, Clara erupted in a spasm which had her clutching at Jake's arm.

'Dry and chesty,' pronounced the doctor, 'that'll be a shilling.' He extracted some lozenges from his tray and wrapped them in a twist of paper.

Clara's eyes widened at the price. The poorest, who couldn't afford proper doctors, sought the street doctors' remedies. But this was not cheap.

'What's in 'em?' asked Jake.

'Mouse foot, herring bone, some parsley and rose water.' He showed his teeth to Clara. Then he guffawed at Jake's expression. 'Don't be alarmed, my boy. I can't be giving away my secret formula, now can I?' He clapped his shoulder with a wink.

'And this works?'

'Yes, my boy, never had any complaints, now if you don't mind—' His eyes focused on an old man with a giant boil on his nose.

Jake moved off, muttering, 'Never had any complaints because they're all dead.'

Clara tugged at his sleeve. Around the corner, she popped one of the lozenges into her mouth. It was revolting, like mint-flavoured tar, and she almost spat it out, but it had been so costly that she persevered. She felt a slow warming in her chest, a gentle easing of her lungs.

'If you're ready,' said Jake, 'we'll now find work.'

Clara took his hand. Jake always had a plan. He was so determined that they would regain a good life that she thought he might bring it about through the sheer power of his will.

In the end, it took a week for them both to find situations, neither of which were ideal. But it was a start. Clara was helping out on a second-hand clothes stall, where she was at least able to replace her rags. It meant standing on her feet all day, trying to entice the passers-by, who mostly wanted to sell rather than acquire. Mrs

Turner, who recognised Clara's commercial potential, dressed her hair in ribbons, and costumed her in the best wares to attract customers. It almost made Clara feel like a lady again.

Jake had started on a fish stall, gutting and skinning all day. He reeked of it when he returned, stumbling with exhaustion. 'Tomorrow will be better,' he would gasp, before collapsing in their only chair.

At the end of their first month, they sat on the bed in the glow of the candle, counting their earnings. The fire belched smoke with each gust of wind that shook the panes, but thanks to the street doctor's remedy and the relative warmth of the room, Clara's cough was now just a slight wheeze.

Jake kept all their coins in the yellow leather purse, tied around his neck. It never left his person, not even while he slept. Now it was open on the bed, coppers and even a few gold coins gleaming in the light. He pushed his hands through the pile with a giggle of pure boyish delight which softened the hard line of his jaw, and then returned it to the purse and tucked it into his shirt.

'This is our future. We shall never, ever be poor again. You have my promise.'

That night, as Clara dozed against Jake's shoulder, it was the first time that a new life felt within her reach.

Although she had never doubted Jake when he said things would get better, it had been such a long time since Hampstead Street, and Mother and Father and Dorothy, that it had started to take on the dimensions of a dream, indistinct and unreal.

She wondered what Uncle Robert would make of them, if he could see them now. He would pass them by on the street without recognition, she was sure of it. So quick was he to wash his hands of them, it had seemed mere days between Father's funeral and Uncle Robert leading them through the workhouse gates. After the first month there, hands bleeding from the carbolic of the laundry room, stomachs griping from the terrible food, feet frozen when bigger children stole their shoes, Jake determined that anything else would be preferable. He watched, and waited, and noticed that the driver of the milk wagon sometimes neglected to shut the gates properly when he made his dawn delivery. They slipped out one frosty spring morning, with nowhere to go.

It was frightening to flee across the crunchy grass, hand in hand, but also exhilarating after the past month of unceasing labour and casual beatings from the staff and other children. The trees were budding, and warmer weather was on the way, but it was still a shock, an enormous shock, to huddle under railway arches and in stinking alleys. As Jake said every night, when Clara cried and her cough became worse and worse, 'At least we are free. And things will get better. I promise you, I will find a way.' His words were her anchor, the only safe thing in the storm around them.

Clara heard the noise first. The room was in darkness, but the thin curtains allowed a seam of moonlight to spill across the bed. Jake was breathing softly beside her alongside the window. At first she thought it was another rat. Some of them were as big as terriers. But then a shadow blocked the moonlight and whoever it was began patting all over Jake's person.

'Wha—?' He woke with a gasp.

'Where is it?' said a Scottish voice. 'I know it's here somewhere. I've looked everywhere else. Give it up, my boy.'

With a cluck of triumph, Mrs Clayburn snipped the purse from Jake's neck and turned to the window to inspect her prize. 'Now where'd a couple of snipes like you be gettin' a sum like this? Not cleanin' fish, I'll wager.'

Jake went to snatch it from her, but for a large woman she was surprisingly quick.

'Give it back!' he shouted, and made a lunge, which left him tumbled on the floor. 'You thief! I'll call the police!'

'Police, you say?' She turned to him, silhouetted against the curtains. 'Would you not think they'd be interested in finding the rightful owner of this fine purse, hmm? No, my boy,' she said with a satisfied sigh, and tucked the purse into her bodice, 'I'll keep it safe. Be grateful it was me. A couple like you, spending money the way you have around here, attracts all the wrong sort. Could have had your pretty throat cut.' She paused in the doorway. 'You have until breakfast to get out.' And with that, she was gone.

Clara was too shocked even to cry. Jake just stared at the window and the distant, uncaring moon.

They were back on the street again. With no address, they could not work. She would end up like Martha, crawling among the beggars, hoping for a few tea leaves.

But when Jake turned to her, his expression was not one of rage or grief, but of granite-hard determination.

'What is it?' Clara managed to whisper, afraid of the answer.

He rummaged in the front of his britches for a moment and she turned away.

'Look,' he said, and extracted another purse, much smaller than the yellow leather one but still healthily plump. 'I have learned that a canny gentleman will always carry two.'

She covered her mouth to stifle the shout of glee. They could get another room … somewhere with a lock on the door.

'I can go back to the fish market,' he said, 'and you to the clothes stall, but only for a short while. We will earn enough to get a better room, and then we will find better situations for both of us. It will take some time, but we will be back where we belong. Eventually.'

Clara considered this vision of the future. She would be an old maid by the time they became respectable. She thought back to Hampstead Street, and all they had taken for granted there. She thought of the prosperous visitors, and the dinners filled with laughter and wine and candlelight. And she thought, *There must be a better way.*

'Jake,' she said, 'back home, who were the richest of Father's friends?'

'Why, the bankers, of course,' he said, leaning back, hands behind his head.

'Well, why should we not follow their example?'

He sat forward, eyes sharp. 'What do you mean? We cannot set up a bank.'

'No, we cannot. But we know plenty of people who need to borrow money, whom the banks will not serve, whom even the Jews will not serve, because they are too poor.'

'Money-lending?' he said, with a grimace. 'You suggest we lend money? To poor people? They'll never be able to pay it back!'

'We'll lend to people like us, working people, who just need a hand. You and I could repay a small loan, if the interest were low enough. Is it not worth some consideration?'

He was leaning back again, staring at the ceiling. She could almost hear the gears in his mind working. All he said was, 'Hmm, I shall sleep on it.'

She took her place beside him, tingling with a hopeful trepidation.

Chapter 3

'Housewives, who'd have thought it?'

Two months later, and Jake was counting their takings for the day. True enough, and contrary to what Clara had expected, almost all of their customers were women, desperate for housekeeping money. The condition was that they leave an item of value – a pocket watch, a locket, a silver comb – returned when they repaid the loan. Their new room on Shelby Street (complete with lock on the door) was becoming cluttered with the collateral, and their landlord, Mr Teckman, had already decreed that they must find a place of business or vacate the room.

Given the nature of their clientele, it made most sense for Clara to front the operation, with Jake keeping the books. At first, people couldn't believe that such young people were able to run a business, and they had a few unfriendly exchanges with the established competition. They were robbed twice, but then hired protection in the form of Max, a former boxer, and were left in peace.

'Mrs Ketteridge is late. Their loan was due last week,' said Jake with a yawn, tired eyes blinking at the ledger. He still put in a full day's work on the fish stall. 'She needs a visit.'

'Oh, Jake, but it's nearly Christmas.' She put aside the sock that she was darning. Both of them wore socks that were more hole than sock and their feet were always freezing. Clara's idea of paradise was warm feet. The fire sputtered but she daren't put on more coal until morning. 'Can't we leave her until New Year? Her baby is ill and—'

Jake looked up sharply and put aside his quill. 'Christmas? Do we get a day off? No, we do not. Then why should our customers get to make merry at our expense? We lent them the money in good faith. The least they can do is repay us in kind. And on time.' He shut the ledger and rubbed his eyes, smearing his cheek with ink. 'You mustn't get involved with them and their problems. Mark me, they will drag you down.'

It gave him the look of a small boy again, and she smudged the ink away with her handkerchief. But he was becoming a man. A businessman, and a good one. All his energy, body and soul, was devoted to the goal of bettering themselves. He was doing it for her, for both of them, so they would never be hungry or cold again. She knew that and appreciated how hard it was. But still, there were times when it seemed that his heart had turned to copper.

This is temporary. The struggle is so hard. When things get easier, he'll turn back into the warm, caring individual than I know so well. I am sure of it.

'I will visit her tomorrow. Now sleep, brother.'

'Max will go with you. It's not safe on your own.'

Clara set off in heavy rain the next morning with the hulking, snuffling figure of Max by her side. As wide as he was tall, he cleared a path for her through the crowds. The snow had turned to dirty slush, which splashed her legs every time a carriage drove past. A sandwich board man passed her, advertising soap. Their steps turned off into the cramped, filthy alleys of the slums. Here were no fine carriages, no hawkers of sweets; just the smell of sewage and cabbage, the flutter of dingy washing overhead, and the sound of crying babies.

Clara didn't dare share with Jake that she not only was involved with their customers' problems, but she knew them intimately. Mrs Gilvin had terrible gout that forced her to give up work as a flower-seller, with six mouths to feed, including a perpetually drunken husband. Mrs Bainbridge's husband had worked on one of the river barges. He drowned one night when he was drunk, after running up debts with a very nasty money-lender known for smashing the kneecaps of his delinquent clients. Mrs Lee had had three children in four years, all of whom developed the whooping cough, yet she had no money for the doctor. And then there was Mrs Ketteridge. Three of her four children had died of malnutrition, and it looked like the last one was going the same way. Her house had been flooded again by the annual Thames overflow. They had nowhere else to go, so were living in the damp, mouldy remains of the house. Clara had not told Jake that Mrs Ketteridge had left no item of collateral for her loan.

Clara stepped over an open sewer, the corner of her shawl over her nose, to arrive at her door during a welcome break in the downpour.

'Wait outside,' she instructed Max.

Mrs Ketteridge – Lila – was sweeping the floor, with her baby, Elsie, swaddled in a dirty blanket in her arm. The walls of the house were stained to a height of two feet from the flooding. When she saw Clara, her lined face went the colour of Elsie's blanket. She leaned the broom against the wall, just as it started to rain again.

'You'd better come in,' she said.

The smell of river mud and decay was overwhelming. Little light penetrated the filmy windows, whose frames were all stuffed with wads of paper. The sputtering fire in the corner created more steam than heat. A rapid series of sneezes emanated from Elsie's blanket.

'There, little one,' cooed Lila. 'That's better, ain't it?'

'How are things, Lila?' Clara asked, dreading the answer. 'Has Dick managed to find work?'

Lila's husband had been nearly blinded in a foundry accident six months previously. Since then, he had struggled to stay with anything for long.

'There's word of needing vegetable porters in the market.'

These sturdy fellows carried heavy baskets of produce on their heads. It was hard to imagine little Dick Ketteridge managing one of those, but he was game for anything. This was why, despite the lack of collateral, Clara had agreed the loan. Dick and Lila were fighters. Despite the awful hand they had been dealt, they were not giving up. Dick was sober. Lila did the best she could to make a home. They deserved a break.

And here she was, about to pull the rug from under them.

This could so easily have been me and Jake. Had we not found that dying man in the alley that night, everything could have been different. Money changes all. And we will never be without it again.

'You know why I am here …' she began, making a determined effort to be the businesswoman Jake needed her to be.

Dick came in then, feeling his way around the familiar contours of the room. 'Lila,' he said, 'do we have a visitor?'

'It's Clara Marley,' she said without emotion, 'come about the loan.' Elsie started to sneeze again.

'Lila tells me there might be work for you in the market,' said Clara, trying to find some shred of hope to discuss.

'Aye,' he said with a sigh, resting beside the fire. 'I reckon so. Pass me the wee one, Lila, let me warm her.' And he took Elsie in his arms. 'Should be able to pay you back in full next week.'

'Next week?'

'Aye,' he said, 'I reckon so. With a bit of luck. How's my lucky girl?' He kissed Elsie's forehead.

Clara did a rapid calculation of the extra interest they would need to charge for that week. And what Jake would say about the delay.

'You know, the loan came due last week. There will be more interest to pay.' She kneaded her cold fingers. 'I'm sorry. It's just business.'

Lila looked helplessly from her to Dick.

'You'll have it all next week,' said Dick, raising his filmy eyes. 'Dick Ketteridge pays his debts. I'm asking you to believe me, which I know isn't how things work in your business. I'm asking you to trust me. Can you do that? For another week?'

Max poked his head in the door with an enquiring glance but Clara shook her head and he withdrew.

Dick wasn't begging, and he wasn't pleading. He was making a statement of fact. Clara found herself completely undone by his simple dignity in such awful circumstances. Whatever work he got, she knew, the money would go towards paying back the loan, rather than on food for Elsie, now asleep in her father's arms. She felt like a slug at the bottom of a drain. She and Jake were better off in comparison, but they had nothing to spare these people.

Jake had warned her not to get involved, and now she understood why. Her heart was breaking, just when she needed to harden it.

'Next week, then.' She rose and fled out into the rain, Max scurrying on his short legs to keep up.

How on earth will I tell Jake? she wondered.

His reaction was utterly predictable.

'You agreed *what*?'

31

Tired, his feet aching, and stinking of fish, he slumped down beside the fire and glared at Clara. She poured him a cup of stewed tea, without milk.

'I'm sorry. I know you're right, but—'

'I am right. You are putting us at risk with your sentimentality. We are not running a charity for destitute women. The sooner you realise that, the better. Or we will find ourselves right back in the gutter.'

She had never heard such coldness in his voice before.

'Yes, Jacob.' She rarely used his full name, but he suddenly seemed much older. By the candlelight, she had a vision of how he would look in middle age.

Unsettled and close to tears, she said, 'What shall we do?'

'We shall collect the payment in full next week and never lend to them again. That is a new rule. No one ever gave us a second chance, and we shall give none to others. Everyone knows where they stand. That's good business.'

'But, Jacob, what about kindness? Shouldn't we care about what happens to others worse off than ourselves? What about … humanity?' Her words sounded silly and empty, when they were in a struggle for sheer survival. Maybe such things were luxuries, to be afforded only when one had a full belly, clean sheets, and warm feet. Her own were wet and freezing. She pushed them closer to the fire, but it was giving out more light than heat.

'I ask you, when did anyone ever show that to us? We would have died in that workhouse, like so many others, and no one would have shed one tear. You see those fine ladies and gentlemen hold their noses and step over the starving. What about the kindness and humanity for two orphaned children? No, Clara. Your feeling is misplaced. Everyone in this world looks after themselves, and none other. That is what it takes to survive. And I mean for us to survive.'

'But,' she said, worn down by the weight of his arguments, 'what about at Christmas time? Is that not a special time, when people come together to share what they have? The one time of the year when we can care for others, whatever our own struggles … and whatever our wounds from the past?'

He said nothing for a moment, but if anything, his face grew even harder. 'Christmas. Don't talk to me about Christmas. Religious nonsense dressed up in sentiment. Humbug, I say. Pure humbug.'

PART II: THE MIDDLE

Chapter 4

Chapter 4

Clara stood in the street and eyed her handiwork with satisfaction. The window of Mr Quoit's toy shop glowed. There was barely any space between the jumble of carved boats, the bucket of tin whistles and the stand of wooden swords, yet all gave way to the magnificence of the doll's house which took centre stage in the display. Now that she handled the window displays, Clara could indulge her study of the doll's house, the same as before. Now, instead of a blinding pain, the sight of it produced a dull, persistent ache in her heart. Despite the hefty price tag, it had sold many times over, and Mr Quoit always ensured that the carpenter provided a new one in time for Christmas every year. Her dream was to own it one day.

There were moments when she wished that some genie would shrink her to mouse size, so she could live in it with Mama and Papa again – and Jacob, of course.

He was so busy these days, having taken over

the running of the lending business from her, that they only saw each other at breakfast. It was their hectic time of year. As Christmas approached, many of their debtors spent too much – mostly on drink – and worked too little, recovering from it. Jacob worked even harder as the holiday drew near. She worried for him, as he often took dinner at the Lion's Head and then carried on working into the night. He was so thin, compared to the solid little boy he had been. She felt it was time to give up the lending business. The competition had become more intense recently. Even with protection, they could expect to be threatened and even robbed on a regular basis. And she could no longer stomach the visits to customers, taking money from those less well off than themselves. Jacob would say, 'The reason they're less well off is that they're not willing to do the things necessary to get on in this world.' Although she knew he was right, she sensed that he was ready to move on too. There was a new weariness in his gait, a stoop in his shoulders from hours spent over the ledgers. Now that they could afford two rooms, at a better address just above the toy shop, more things became possible. They had come so far in only a matter of years; their time as beggars was like a terrible nightmare, and the time before that – at their childhood home – like a beautiful dream. Now she was a working woman, both times seemed as insubstantial to Clara as a will-o'-the-wisp.

Snow was just beginning to fall, the sort of fluffy, delicate flakes that turned slowly through the lamplight, frosting the pavements and the shops lining Percy Street, and softening the clop of the horses' hooves. Customers spilled out of the door of Mr Quoit's, arms laden with gaily wrapped packages for lucky children. She thought of the ones they had left behind in the workhouse and shuddered. A group of ragged poor children were always clustered around the window, noses running, smearing the dimpled glass with their grubby hands. Dreaming of toys they would never touch, much less possess. The little one with the crutch was there with his gaggle of siblings, too small to see the full display, so his brother lifted him up. The small one beamed with wonder.

'A perfect Christmas Eve,' she said to herself, pulling her bonnet down over her ears.

Only she found she was not alone. Mr Woodburn, who had the tea stall opposite, was at her side with a steaming cup. Right on time. They had fallen into a routine, as she had stepped outside into the cold to perfect her displays in the dark of the afternoon. Everything about him was large, from his square feet planted in rubber boots to his crown of wild black hair, now adorned with melting snowflakes. His features were too large to be handsome, overhung with heavy brows, but they suited him. And he always seemed to be smiling. She found him a cheering presence.

'Indeed it is. But why do you sound sad?' he asked, handing her the cup. Mr Quoit was too busy serving a customer to bother about her chattering for a few minutes. Her imaginative, sumptuous displays, and eye for style and colour, had increased his trade since she joined as a shop girl six months ago.

'I am missing my family. My parents died when we were children, so there is only my brother and me.' The tea cup warmed her hands, her nose tickled by the fragrant steam.

'I am sorry.'

'It was a long time ago.'

'Aye, but Christmas is a family time.' He sipped his tea, brows now collecting snowflakes too. 'It must be very hard. I'd be lost without mine.'

'Your wife and children?'

'Nay, lassie.' He shook some snow from his hair. 'My two brothers, and their brood. After we're done with the Christmas trade, we all meet at the end of the month at my parents' house in the Borders for Hogmanay, where the bairns can run riot. There's a good dozen of us in total, with games and more food than anyone can eat.'

'That sounds absolutely … wonderful.' She had a wistful vision of a crowd around a roaring fire, singing songs and indulging in superstitions to usher in the new year, the smell of roast meat in the air competing with bowers of greenery. Then she thought of Christmas with Jacob. He considered it to be another working day, although she might be able to persuade him to put down his quill long enough for lunch at the Lion's Head. There was no question of exchanging gifts, however modest.

'There I go again, making you sad. It wasn't my intention.'

'It is not your fault, Mr Woodburn. Really it is not. This time of year just brings back lots of memories.'

'Call me Tom. It's Thomas, but that's my pa's name.'

'Tom,' she held out her hand, 'I'm Clara, Clara Belle Marley.'

There followed a hollow silence which she did not know how to fill. His black eyes rested on her, not intrusive, just interested.

'Business is … good?' she asked finally, unable to think of anything else to say.

'Aye, always in cold weather, but really all year there's a demand for tea. The English are mad for it!'

He chuckled long and deep. 'I have big plans for the new year. More shops, hire a few people. My plan is to be on every street corner in the borough.'

It was an ambitious plan, which would take capital. She filed the knowledge away.

'Tom's Teas?' She smiled.

'Not bad at all, lassie, not bad!' He raised his cup to her. 'I shall consult my chief business adviser, Bertie. What do you think, old chap?'

Sure enough, there was a mixed breed in a patchwork of colours, resting in the warmth of the tea urn. It raised its head on hearing his name, wagged a soggy tail, then rested again on his paws.

'Bertie approves.' He grinned, showing white teeth like dominoes. 'Miss Clara, would you do me the honour of dining with me sometime?'

She sputtered, then handed him back the cup and smoothed her skirt, feeling wholly unsettled. 'Well,' she said, 'must get back to work. Thank you for the tea.' And she fled indoors.

She felt his mystified eyes follow her all the way.

When Clara climbed the stairs to their rooms above the shop later that day, the unsettled feeling still clung to her. She lit the fire and rested in the chair beside it, staring into the flames to find an answer there. Clara did not have suitors. While fronting the lending business, she never encountered anyone suitable; most men she dealt with despised her while needing her services. She had developed a carapace of indifference, had to learn to distinguish between the truly needy and the simply indolent. 'You are hard for a woman,' she had heard, more times than she could count, uttered with pleading or contempt. And then in the past six months of working at Quoit's, she was barely able to keep up with the workload let alone a suitor, and climbed the stairs every night, exhausted.

To converse with a man who was not a customer of some kind was a novelty. She recalled Mr Woodburn's – Tom's – black eyes on her. He was looking at her in such an unaccustomed way, she did not know what to make of it. And why was he not married, at his age, with a brood of his own? He was obviously on his way to being successful. Why had some Scottish 'lassie' not snapped him up?

She rose and stared into the stained looking glass above the fire. Her skin was unlined, her hair warmly golden in the light, but her eyes … her eyes were old. She had seen and done things that would shock someone like Tom if he knew. How could she ever communicate what she and Jacob had been through to get where they were? How could someone like him – from a large, happy family – understand?

With a sigh, she leaned her head on her arms against the mantle and let the fire warm her belly.

What is to become of me? Clara had always assumed that her life would be just like Mother's – running a home, raising children, with a husband to provide for them. This was what normal women did. For the first time, she was confronted with the truth: she would never have a life like her mother's. It felt like she had swallowed a stone.

What would Mother say if she could see me now? A shop girl with no prospects of a match?

Staring again into the looking glass, she saw herself twenty years hence – grey, lined, dressed all in black, still keeping house for Jacob.

Her eyes travelled to the uncurtained window overlooking Percy Street. On a whim, she opened the window and leaned out. Tom was still in front of his shop, clapping his arms to keep warm, while Bertie snoozed at his feet.

Before she could think, she called down. 'Tom!' The snow was falling in a heavy curtain now, deadening the sound. She had to call a second time. 'Tom! Up here!'

He came into the street and waved, a black-topped shape in the white.

'Yes!' she called. 'I say yes!'

His white smile glowed even through the snow. 'Have a merry Christmas, Miss Clara!'

'And a happy new year to you!'

She shut the window and hugged herself. What would Mother have said, to see her yelling down to a shopkeeper in the street? It was scandalous. She hugged herself again and smiled at the thought, then felt the customary tickle in her chest as the cold air from outside lodged itself there. She fought the urge to cough, then gave in to it, let it cough itself out. She never had a cough in the before time, when her mother would have been there to comfort her. Now she had to comfort herself.

Well, Mother isn't here. I can't do things her way, so I have to do them in my own.

When Jacob came in, she was asleep beside the dying fire. Immediately she could tell something had happened, by the way he leapt across the room and pulled her from her seat.

'I have done it, Clara! I am, as of today, apprenticed as a book-keeper!'

'Oh, Jacob, that is marvellous news! Which establishment?'

He could not contain his excitement, pacing the

small confines of the room. 'Old Fezziwig's firm. He's had it for years and years, very well established. Very good reputation. I was lucky to get the position. Such news!' He spun her around.

'Such news! Oh, Jacob, let us go out and celebrate! A porter or two wouldn't go amiss tonight. And perhaps a steamed pudding? It's Christmas Eve!'

But he settled into the chair and poked the fire. 'No, my dear. Such good fortune should only make us more prudent. I've known many a debtor who only became such after a windfall.'

She took the chair opposite, somewhat deflated but still buoyed by his news. 'You are right, brother, of course.' She paused, the words bubbling inside her. 'I have a bit of news of my own to share.'

'Oh yes?' he said, eyes still on the fire.

'I've been asked to dinner by Tom – Mr Woodburn, who has the tea stall across the street.'

Jacob looked up sharply. 'Tea stall? How did we meet? Where does he come from?'

Flustered, she said, 'We got chatting while I did my displays. He comes from Scotland, two brothers and a big family.'

'Why is he not married yet?'

'I—don't know. Perhaps, like you, he has been focused on his business. And he has ambitions to open many more shops in the borough.' She guessed that this would soften his response.

'Does he now?' He turned thoughtful. 'That will require capital.'

'That's what I thought. Perhaps you could advise him when the time is right?' Clara sat back, relieved. She never enjoyed incurring his displeasure. Lately it could be triggered by the smallest thing. It seemed that, the better their circumstances, the more fearful he became of losing them. She wanted him to sample some of life's pleasures with his hard-earned coins, but he would not hear of it. *What else was money for?* she wondered, but it was clear that Jacob took a different view. He was building a fortress of money around the two of them, to keep them safe, to give them the life he had promised every night in the workhouse, every night in the freezing alleyway. She understood why he needed to do that. She never wanted to be poor again either.

But, she thought, *a fortress is also designed to keep everyone else out.*

She pulled closer to the fire and studied her brother's features in the dying light. None of the boy remained. All that had been burnt away by their struggle, leaving an immovable determination to survive. Sometimes she mourned the playful, good-natured scamp he had been, always laughing and ready with a prank.

But that Jacob was gone. This was Jacob now, on his way to becoming a man of business, and no one's fool.

Despite the good news of the day, and the festive sounds from the street, she felt a chill melancholy steal over her.

'Good night, brother,' she said, and kissed his forehead, 'and happy Christmas.'

Chapter 5

Three months later, and winter's icy grip was slowly easing. Days were longer, nights not quite so bitter. Clara longed for the spring, her favourite season, even more than summer, when the heat brought the reek of rotting fruit in addition to the usual odours. No, spring was perfect; as the air warmed, her seasonal cough abated somewhat. And the flowers were so fresh, so brave to bloom even through layers of snow and ice. They were a promise of better days. A few primroses in a glass on her dressing table turned their sweet faces to her as she fussed with her bonnet.

She wrenched it off in frustration. 'Oh, what shall I wear?' she asked the flowers, but they just basked in their effortless beauty. She and Jacob were dining for the first time with Jacob's fellow apprentice, Ebenezer Scrooge, and his fiancé. She was sure to be stylish and elegant, and Clara quailed at the thought of falling short. Jacob had quickly become friends with Ebenezer, who was as poor as they were, but showing signs of real acumen. She sensed that Jacob had found a kindred spirit and rejoiced in it. He went to work each morning with a spring in his step, and spread his wages on the table each week, laughing and running the coins through his hands as if he could not believe his luck. It was the first time since Hampstead Street that he had made a friend.

'Are we ready, my sweet?' asked Jacob. He stood behind her, hands on her shoulders, as she scowled at herself in the dressing table mirror.

'What if they don't like me?' Her stomach ached, her limbs felt cold. It had been so long since she had met anyone new socially, except Tom, of course. But she was as comfortable with him now as with her old boots, which she noticed were stained with muck. 'I must polish my boots!' She sat down with some boot black and a brush and scraped away at them.

'Of course they will like you!' He sat beside her and took the brush from her. With a few long strokes, her footwear was redeemed. 'You are charming and witty. And they are like us, no airs and graces. I promise. Now we must go.' He raised her up. 'Ebenezer is nothing if not punctual.'

She looked into his eyes, which shone with good humour and excitement. Like the old Jacob, a glimmer of the boy he had been. Clara sensed they stood on the threshold of great changes. For good or ill, she could not tell.

She tucked a primrose into the ribbon of her bonnet and turned to him. 'I am ready.'

The fug of smoke, beer and sweat hit her as they entered the Lion's Head. The tables were full of diners. Swirling among them were harassed barmaids with several tankards clutched in each fist. Above the noise, Jacob called, 'Over there!' He led her towards the corner, where a tall, thin young man stood waving.

They ducked behind a partition where it was slightly quieter.

Jacob shook Ebenezer's hand and said, 'May I present my sister, Clara Belle?'

'Delighted to meet you.' He pumped her hand. Clara's first impression was of bright, friendly eyes in an almost skeletal face. She had not seen anyone so thin since the poorest beggars in the alley. But then he smiled and was transformed. 'And this is my fiancé, Belle.' His smile glowed with pride and affection.

Clara turned her attention to the petite blonde woman sitting quietly at the table and immediately realised she need not have worried about her attire. Although her clothes, like that of Jacob and Ebenezer, were frayed and much mended out of necessity, Clara recognised Belle's dress from the second-hand clothes stall. It was one she had modelled to tempt passers-by. Clearly ill at ease, Belle fussed with her sleeve. Whatever anxiety Clara had about the meeting melted away. She could have been Belle. She was Belle.

Looking past the awful dress, Clara saw a delicate beauty. There was a warmth about her, an air of kindness, a calmness which drew Clara to sit beside her.

She took both her hands. 'Clara Belle and Belle. It was fate that we should meet. I have a feeling that we shall be great friends.' Like Jacob, it had been many years since she had a friend.

Belle beamed at her, and Clara understood Ebenezer's attachment, despite her obvious poverty. 'I would like that. Very much.'

'Excellent!' exclaimed Ebenezer. 'Let us eat and drink – barmaid, four flagons of ale!'

The woman sloshed their drinks onto the table and Ebenezer raised his tankard and smacked it against Jacob's. 'To friendship!'

Jacob gave him a long look which Clara could not read.

'To friendship,' echoed Jacob, tankard raised. 'Friendship everlasting.'

The remains of the meal littered their plates. If anything, the noise of their fellow drinkers grew louder as the hour drew later. Clara, despite being on her feet all day at Mr Quoit's, was so enjoying herself that she did not notice the time.

The barmaid set glasses of porter between them and Clara savoured the sweet, silky feel of it going down her throat. Jacob and Ebenezer had their heads together, one dark, one fair. *They are as close as brothers.* Slightly lost in visions of being chosen as a bridesmaid, she turned to Belle.

'When do you and Ebenezer plan to marry?'

With a sigh, Belle replied, 'Oh, likely not for ages. Not until we can make a proper home together. Ebenezer has decreed it.' She looked over at her fiancé with a mixture of fondness and frustration.

'You would marry sooner?'

'Yes! All I want is a roof and four walls. Ebenezer and I, that's what makes a home. But he feels differently.' She folded her hands, eyes down. 'He has grand plans.'

'But they will take time?'

Belle nodded. 'Do not misunderstand: I am proud of his ambition. I too would like a better life.' Her eyes went to Ebenezer again. 'But I am accustomed to doing without. I would like for us to strive together. But he will not hear of it.'

'Well, then we must find pleasant diversions for ourselves while his plans take shape.'

Belle eyed her. 'I do believe that those plans involve your brother.'

Back in their rooms, Clara turned thoughtful as she poked the dying embers of the fire. A chill wind had followed them home, like a ghost of winter. It whistled through the window frames and caused the chimney to belch.

Jacob took the opposite chair, cravat undone. 'You're very quiet. Did you enjoy the evening?'

She sat back on her heels. 'Very much. I can see why you have become fond of Ebenezer, and Belle is a delight. She said something interesting.' A pause. 'She talked of Ebenezer's grand plans, and said that you were involved.'

He looked away. 'He shares far too much with that girl.'

'She is his fiancé! Of course he shares plans with her. I would expect no less from whomever I marry. And from my brother.'

His face clouded, eyes dark as the soot from the fire. 'I am not at all sure that she is right for him. She brings nothing to the marriage, no dowry at all.'

'They are in love!'

'Yes, and try paying the bills with that. Marriage is a business transaction like any other, an exchange of goods and services. You should understand that.'

Something in his voice chilled her more than the draught. 'Surely that is not all! Oh, Jacob, you wouldn't share this opinion with Ebenezer, would you? He looks up to you so, like an elder brother.'

But he had clearly closed the subject. He rose and stretched. 'You want to know our plans? Old Fezziwig is finished. In time, we could take over the company as a going concern.'

She stood beside him, hands on his arms. 'But he has been so good to you and Ebenezer.' Fezziwig's Christmas parties were legendary. He spent at least three pounds on food, drink, and entertainment for his staff.

Jacob shook her off. 'He belongs to the past. We are the future. Just think of it, Clara! Scrooge & Marley.' His eyes shone behind his round spectacles. 'I can already see the shingle we shall have.'

His excitement was contagious and it dispelled some of her doubts. Jacob knew best when it came to business matters. She had not imagined anything so ambitious. And she had no doubt at all that her brother and Ebenezer would achieve it together.

'But why does it have to be at the expense of a good friend? Can you not find another way?'

Jacob shrugged and turned away. 'It's nothing personal. Just business.'

Chapter 6

Tom arrived right on time to collect her on an unseasonably warm May Day, atop a little cart smelling of tea leaves, pulled by a pony who swivelled its ears at every street sound. The morning sun glinted off the glossy enamel shopfronts of Percy Street; the flower-sellers had long set up their pitches, competing to offer the freshest violets. The smell of fresh fish mingled with manure. A water cart passed by, sluicing the gutters and damping the road to control the choking dust that would rise later.

Tom jumped down to help her, just as the horse snickered and tossed its head. 'Now, Elspeth, this is Clara Belle. We're going out for the day.'

'Elspeth?' The horse regarded Clara with wary interest.

'After my sainted grandmother. Same profile.'

Elspeth snuffled at Clara's pocket, where an apple was secreted. 'Is this what you're looking for?'

The horse munched it down in two bites, blinked, and then faced forward with a stamp of impatient hooves.

'Clever Clara. That's her favourite, although she is partial to a wee dram.' He chuckled at her surprise. 'Nah, that'll be me.'

He stowed the picnic basket and lifted her onto the seat. Although not a small woman, she felt light as a dandelion in his grip.

They set off at a smart clip in the warming air, weaving through fine carriages with liveried footmen, hansom cabs pulled by plodding nags, and reeking dust carts piled high with grey refuse and grey people. Everywhere the horses jostled for space with people. From up ahead, a cry of pain and a stream of curses from someone caught by stray hooves.

Their destination: the Common. The open spaces and fresh air attracted families from all over, desperate to escape the noxious, disease-ridden soup of the slums or, for the wealthier, an excuse to show off their fine carriages and Sunday clothes. On a day like this, half of London would be out for a stroll.

Clara recalled Jacob's scowl when she announced her intention to go on today's outing with Tom.

'What news of his expansion plans?' He looked up briefly from the drawing he was studying.

Jacob only ever asked about Tom's business, never about Clara's feelings for him. But Jacob was completely preoccupied with the opening of the new Scrooge & Marley premises, such that Clara felt she could say almost anything and receive a grunt in reply. The only thing that made a difference was talking about business – theirs, competitors', the state of the market. This was when their connection was strengthened again, for Clara still had a deep interest in the new business, and was very excited for both Jacob and Ebenezer, whom she was coming to think of as another brother. And she had been spending a lot of time with Belle – patient, lovesick Belle. Her dearest wish was that early success for Scrooge & Marley could bring about wedding bells. But Clara knew these things took time. Years, even.

Tom had not made her privy to his progress, which did not trouble her. It either meant that things were happening apace, or they were not, and she would find out when he was ready. She was in no hurry.

'We haven't discussed it lately.'

Jacob's scowl deepened but he said nothing. He closed the portfolio and stood to kiss her on the cheek. 'Don't wait up for me. I will dine at the inn with Ebenezer.'

Picnic basket on her arm, bonnet tied against the

sun, she watched him go. He hadn't said how pretty she looked for quite a while now.

The sun beamed down on her bonnet, and she was glad of the shade from its brim. Tom hummed as Elspeth made steady progress along the thoroughfares, joining the throngs headed for the Common. They had been travelling in not entirely comfortable silence when she became aware of his agitation. It showed a little in the way he handled the reins, a little in the set of his chin. With a shock, she became fully aware of just how well she knew him, and what this outing's true purpose was. The thought came through clearly: *He is going to ask for my hand.*

All at once she was very warm, so loosened the bow at her neck. 'Goodness, this weather! Glorious!' She produced a fan to move the air around her face, but it did little to cool.

Up ahead was an Italian ice-seller. Tom turned Elspeth in his direction. 'How thoughtless of me. We shall have ices under that tree over there and cool off.'

In the shade of a horse chestnut tree, they tethered Elspeth next to a water trough and sank down on the grass to slurp the sweet ices. There was no dignified way to eat them, and soon the tension was broken by wiping sticky drips from their faces.

The silence settled on them again. A tense grin from Tom. She searched for something to distract.

'Who is that over there?'

A small man in a large tweed coat and mangled top hat, far too warm for the weather, was busy opening carriage doors for fine ladies, each time with a bow and sweep of his hat and a hand held out for a coin.

'That's Tweed, used to tailor in it, so that was the only name he had. 'Til his eyesight went, so now he begs.' With a brush of Elspeth's soft nose, he said, 'It can be surprising, sometimes, how quickly people can fall into debt … and never recover.'

Clara wondered, *What would you say if you knew my story?* But she said nothing. Her eyes roamed over a group of army recruiting sergeants, sweating in their tight collars, eyeing up the groups of single men, who eyed them in turn.

Placid donkeys plodded by, topped with squealing children, led by dark men with huge moustaches.

She started to relax amidst all the pageantry, because although it was tawdry and poor, and the plaintive cries of beggars competed with ice-sellers, there was still something … splendid about the spectacle of London at leisure. These open spaces were one of the few places where rich and poor mingled without railings or barriers.

Then Tom turned his eyes on her and her heart pounded. 'Shall we have a photo taken?'

'A photo?'

'Yes, to mark the day.' He pulled her to her feet and lifted her into the trap. 'Over there.' He indicated where a man with a black-draped head gesticulated to an unruly family group whose children were more interested in chasing pigeons.

'You must remain perfectly still!' the photographer pleaded in a strong French accent.

Tom led Elspeth over to within a few feet of him as the family dispersed with a shrug.

'Can you get all three of us?' asked Tom.

'All three …?' asked the photographer with some bemusement.

'Yes, Clara and me and the horse, with the trap, if you please.' Tom climbed up beside Clara and took the reins. Elspeth shook her head.

'The horse must remain perfectly motionless,' said the photographer with a doubtful look.

Tom cleared his throat and tapped the horse lightly with the reins and she became a statue of a pony – completely still, ears high, eyes forward, one hoof poised. Clara put on her most serious face, as did Tom. No one ever smiled in photographs.

The photographer quickly draped his head and

fussed with the camera until a puff of grey smoke from the flash broke the spell and Elspeth stamped, her patience exhausted.

'Give me your address.' And with a final glance at Elspeth, 'Delivery in a week.'

With a click of his tongue, Tom moved the trap on through the crowds, slowly promenading. The sun was at its full height now. The colours, the music, the smells, the mixture of languages all combined with the heat to make Clara light-headed.

'Shall we picnic now?' she suggested.

'Excellent idea.'

Tom made a few turns, avoiding other picnickers, as if searching for the perfect spot, which he found in a quiet corner under some plane trees next to a field of sheep. The animals remained prostrate in the shade at their arrival, chewing.

Clara spread the food out on the blanket; just a few Scotch eggs, some cheese, bread, and apples to share. There was also warm lemonade.

She was searching her mind for small talk when he said, 'Clara, I am making good progress with my plan. I've identified four new premises that I want to take over, all at the same time, to establish myself in the borough.' He paused, an expectant smile on his face.

She put down the piece of bread, slowly.

'Why that's …' She struggled to recover her composure, a lump of bread sticking in her throat. 'Why that's wonderful news! But four at once, isn't that a risk?' With her business head, she was quickly calculating the possible costs and returns. It would be hard work to get it going, and keep it going. And it would take years before it produced a comfortable income – if he didn't go under.

'Yes, it is, but you see … I have another reason for needing to make this a success. And I think you know what that is.' His eyes were soft now. He undid the ribbon of her bonnet. Cool air flowed over her head. She had never been this close to a man before. He smelled of clean sweat, horse, and hot cotton. With her face between his enormous hands, he said, 'I love ya, Clara Belle Marley. If you'll have me, I want to be with you always, have our own brood … build a life together.'

Before she could answer, he went on, holding her hand: 'The thing is … the thing is, you are a lady. Yes, you are, even if you don't have all the trappings of one – yet. I want to give you the life of a lady, the life you deserve. But I am not in that position – not yet.'

She went to speak, to echo pretty much everything Belle had said to Ebenezer, but he cut her off. 'So I am asking for an understanding between us. But it means waiting to fulfil our promise. I will work hard, so hard. I think you know that about me. But I cannot say how long it will take.'

She had to look away from the hopefulness in his eyes. She said nothing for a moment, too overwhelmed by his proposition which filled her heart, and dismayed by the prospect of waiting for the business to provide for their life together.

But as her feelings tumbled over each other, a thought pierced through like a beam of light: *We want to be together. This is not a problem of the heart. This is a business problem, and as such, can be solved. By money.*

'Tom,' she said, still holding his hand. 'I will make an understanding with you on your terms because I love you too.' The realisation came almost as the words left her mouth. It had crept up on her, this feeling of rightness and belonging when she was with him, the way he made her feel ... cherished. They had a future together, of that she was sure. 'But first, you need to know a few things about ... things that happened before we met.'

And so, in quick, matter-of-fact language, she explained how she and Jacob had started and run their business together until they were both able to better themselves. She watched the waves of astonishment wash over his face as she revealed the layers of the past, becoming alarmed that he would feel she had behaved in some unnatural, unwomanly fashion. As she brought the story up to the present, he was looking down at their clasped hands.

Clara waited for him to speak. When he finally raised his head, she saw something more than love; she saw admiration, and she exhaled a long sigh.

'I thought you might … disapprove. It's not exactly, well, usual.'

'It is where I come from. The lasses are at least as canny in business. My old da just handed over his wages to Ma, who ran the housekeeping like the Bank of England. Always the eye for the bargain, had my ma.' He studied her for a moment. 'You remind me a little of her, in fact.'

She forced her mind to focus. He needed capital, it was the only way. She knew better than to offer to help this proud man herself, but she thought he might accept help from someone else.

'I think a conversation with Jacob could be … useful,' she said tentatively.

'I agree. And I want you there. You know him and you know the business.' He kissed her cheek. 'You are an asset, Clara Belle.' And he kissed her other blushing cheek.

Chapter 7

A week later and the weather had turned. Rain spattered the bay window of the Scrooge & Marley premises as Clara and Tom passed under the newly painted sign that was creaking in the wind. The interior smelled of new wood and fresh polish. A large desk nearly filled the window, behind which waited her brother and Ebenezer, hands folded.

In a small vestibule in the back, Clara glimpsed a figure hunched on a high stool over a counting table, smoky candle by his side.

'Who is that, Jacob?'

'Oh, that's the clerk, Perkins.'

The clerk looked up at his name, then bent his head.

It was the first she heard of them employing staff. Things must have moved quickly since they divested Fezziwig of his business. She still felt slightly wrong about that, he was such a nice man, but Jacob had persuaded her that it was the way of such things and 'nothing personal'. It never was 'personal', yet some part of her felt it should be. After all, people needed money to make their lives better – to pay off debts, to buy a place to live … to fund a business. How was that not 'personal'?

She cleared her throat, feeling very strange to introduce her fiancé to her brother to talk about a loan. 'Jacob, Ebenezer, may I present Tom Woodburn, who has a business proposition to discuss with you.'

Tom wore a collar and tie for the first time since they had met, and kept pulling at it. 'Pleased to meet you.' A very wet Bertie huddled under the eaves outside, eyes fixed on his master, and Tom looked like he would prefer to be out there too.

Only now did her brother and Ebenezer stand to shake his hand. 'Sit, please,' invited Ebenezer.

'Clara …?' queried Jacob.

'She is party to our discussion,' said Tom, and grasped her hand. 'With your permission, sir, we have last week made an understanding with each other.' He turned to smile at her. 'It depends on making a success of this business, so you can understand why I am keen to discuss possibilities with you.'

Clara registered the shock on Jacob's face and regretted it immediately. He should not have received the news this way; something she did not want to examine had delayed her speaking to him until it was too late.

Ebenezer was on his feet to pump Tom's hand. 'Well, congratulations, you two.' A veil of sadness hung over him. Clara knew from Belle that he had recently lost his beloved sister, Fan. Ebenezer was inconsolable, irrational in his grief. He blamed his nephew, Fred, only two years old. He blamed Fan's husband for marrying her in the first place. Along with Belle, Fan held the highest place in his heart, which Belle found admirable. But with great attachment comes the pain of great loss. And for Ebenezer, something had changed about him, she was sure of it. Although he appeared gracious, there was something new and hard underneath. With a start, she realised that it reminded her of how Jacob had changed.

Jacob's silence was ominous. He scowled at the desk for a long moment, then collected himself. 'Yes, well that is a conversation for another day.' He poised his quill above a page in his ledger and said, 'We are here to talk about your ... tea business. Tell us about your plans.'

Two hours and several cups of Tom's tea later, Jacob closed the ledger with a long look at Ebenezer.

'That is a very nice drink, indeed,' said Jacob.

'My cousin, Roderick, has a plantation in India,' explained Tom, 'where I get all my stock. So I can verify the quality.'

'If you will excuse us for a moment, I must confer with my partner. Perkins, show our guests through.'

Clara and Tom waited in the other room while Perkins's quill scratched and the low murmur of voices came from behind the desk.

So, this is what it is like to be a customer of Scrooge & Marley. She had never expected to experience it herself. Tom sensed her unease and squeezed her hand. So much depended on this decision. Until this moment, she had not considered the possibility that they could be refused, not by her brother's firm. But now, as she watched him confer with Ebenezer, it was clear that he gave no quarter to Tom's position as her fiancé. This was about risk and reward, pure and simple – for Scrooge & Marley.

With a sign to Perkins, they were invited back in.

Ebenezer said, 'We are willing to loan the full amount for a period of' – he consulted his note – 'two years.'

'At such time, the full sum plus interest becomes due. You understand?' asked Jacob.

'I understand,' said Tom, scratching his head. 'While I am grateful, two years is not long to become established …'

'Those are the terms,' said Ebenezer, making it clear that it was not an opening but a final offer. 'We hear that you are a hard worker.' This with a glance at Clara.

The men began to discuss premises, rent, staff, distribution, but all Clara could think was *two whole years. We have to wait two years.* And she understood very well how Jacob and Ebenezer had come to their decision. She and Tom would have all the capital requested, but would be under intense pressure to succeed. Just as Jacob ran his own affairs.

Jacob said nothing when he first came home that night. When Clara tried to thank him for the loan, and express all her hopes for the business, he rounded on her.

'Are you not content?' he said with such vehemence that she took a step back.

'Why yes, of course I am content.' She hoped it would soothe him but he became more agitated.

'Then why, Clara, why? Why do this? With him?' His eyes were red behind his glasses.

If she didn't know him better, she would think he was in his cups.

'Because, Jacob,' she tried to say as gently as possible, 'I want a home. I want a family. Surely you must as well?'

'We had a family. It was lost to us.'

She watched as all the pain and fear of so long ago stiffened the rapidly ageing planes of his face. It was as if Uncle Robert stood there before them, in Mama's beautiful sitting room, reeking of disinfectant, bustling them out of their own door with less care than he took with the furniture. The astringent disinfectant changed to the putrefaction of the gutter and she felt the chill, like no other chill, a chill that no warmth could alleviate. And now she was back there too, on the filthy pavement with Jacob, wretchedly hungry, as nicely shod feet, swishy perfumed skirts, and sharp-creased trouser legs strode past them, around them. Stepped right over them, as if their bodies were akin to litter, something that really ought to be cleared up and carted off.

And as she looked into his haunted eyes, she read his thoughts distinctly: the odours of pig's trotter and rotten cabbage, fresh blood – a lot of blood. A man, a stranger, gurgling his last, while Jacob rummages through his clothing for the small purse that will save their lives.

'What we did that night ...' she began. 'Most people ...'

'Most people would be in Pauper's Field now, or among the crawlers. Is that what you would prefer?'

'Of course not, but—' Her mind swirled with memories and fragments of thoughts, good and bad, recent and long past. Faces, voices, sounds and smells passed through her as if she were a scrap of muslin in the wind, until finally the random assortment began to coalesce around a single image. The contours of Tom's face emerged from the confusing mass of shapes and colours: solid, real, the beginning of a smile, arms open to receive her. This was home. Wherever he was. This was home.

Jacob's voice cut like a cold blade. 'You made an arrangement. Without discussing it.' He folded his arms in quite righteous indignation. 'As you would say, family discuss such ... things.'

He was absolutely right. 'I was impulsive and thoughtless, and I apologise for being so, and not talking privately with you first.' She took a moment to reflect. *Why did I not? Because I knew he would object, of course, and perhaps have given me ...doubts? No, not that. Hesitation?* She examined her feelings and they had changed not one tiny bit: this was right.

'Jacob.' She put a hand on his arm and he only flinched a little. 'I realise this is unconventional in so many ways that make you uncomfortable. I had no inkling that it was coming. My own feelings weren't even clear to me until he asked me. I hope—'

'Then how can you enter into this agreement with so little thought, for yourself ... for others? Surely it demands more time, more reflection?' He was leaning forward, fists bunched.

'Because,' she said with a shrug, 'as soon as he said the words, it felt right. That is the only thing that mattered.' Even to her ears, it sounded frivolous, but there was nothing frivolous about her feelings for Tom. 'But, Jacob.' It was all so clear. A wonderful future lay ahead, if only he would open his mind. 'I am not doing this to hurt you. What about your future? Once the business is secure, you will be in the position to make an excellent match. A fine house, a caring wife who will give you beautiful children. Can you not see it? We shall have big family Christmases and trips to the seaside ...'

He regarded her with such sadness that the smile froze on her lips.

'You think we can just recreate all that we lost, with a few baubles and sandcastles? It is gone, for ever, the life we had in Hampstead House. I will never allow us to be at risk of that again. I have only one aim in life, and that is to keep you and me safe. I will not be distracted by anything until I have achieved that, until we can never, ever be ruined again. You must ... you must do what you feel is right.'

And there he was, that little boy on the threshold of disaster, as fresh as yesterday.

He looked away and her elation turned to tearfulness. He was sacrificing himself, his happiness, for their security. It was so selfless … but then she paused and recalled the bright, sharp exchanges over Tom's loan that afternoon. Jacob was lit from within as they finessed the contract, doing complex sums in his head faster than Ebenezer. There was only one way to describe it: Jacob was enjoying himself. Business was his calling and yes, it had literally saved their lives, and now it was making them comfortable. But there was also … pleasure there. It was part of his nature, and she felt at that moment that she had not appreciated that fully. What was an interest for her – and a very important one now with Tom's ambitious enterprise – was Jacob's passion.

'I want to be with him. I hope you can find a way to be happy for me.'

He turned away so she barely heard him. 'I think you are making a mistake. I do not believe he is worthy of you. But he has two years to prove otherwise.'

When she shut her bedroom door for the night, he was still at the table, contemplating the fading candle.

There was only one person with whom Clara wanted to share her news: Belle. She would understand all the complex emotions of the situation, and Clara ached to converse with a sympathetic spirit. They met for coffee at Iris's tea room, a small establishment with aspirations to be a dainty retreat for ladies but was too steamy and Miss Iris too lacking in good graces for it to achieve her vision. She decorated everything with a generous waft of pipe ash, but the coffee was good and the cake generous.

As they waited for Iris to bustle through the afternoon rush, Belle said, 'So tell me.'

'Well, I have no ring to show you, but …'

Belle squealed and clapped her hands. 'He asked you, I knew he would! I only just said to Ebenezer the other day that I felt something was going to happen.' She glanced at her left hand. 'I have a little ring, but it makes no difference in the scheme of things.' Looking up brightly. 'Do I dare ask … how long?'

Just as Iris sloshed their coffee onto the table, Clara sighed. 'Two years. Two whole years.'

Belle stirred her coffee and smiled wryly. 'It has already been three for us. The time will pass, you will see. The worst is not knowing for how long … Why do you say two years?'

Clara paused. She and Belle had no secrets, but this was Tom's business. How much should she explain? *Yes, it was Tom's business, but she had opened the door to the funds. And it was their future.* 'You see, Tom has a plan

76

to open tea rooms all over the borough, all around the same time. Like Ebenezer, he will only marry when he can afford to give us a nice home. I know, I know. We have had the same conversation as you, and he is similarly immovable.'

'But, Clara, such ambition! Two years for all that! Very impressive, but where in the world can you raise the money to get it started?'

Clara was silent, just let her expression answer the question.

'Oh, Clara,' breathed Belle. 'I utterly understand why, but you realise the reputation they are gaining for themselves?'

Success at any cost. 'Yes. Yes, I do. But he is my brother, and Ebenezer his best friend.'

Belle shook her head. 'I envy you, but I fear for you at the same time. In case anything should go wrong … where would that leave your plans?'

Clara had, of course, had the same thoughts, but it was disconcerting to hear them expressed aloud by her closest friend, and this turned to mild annoyance. 'I have faith in Tom, and in my brother and Ebenezer. And they believe in us.'

Jacob's words came back to her: *I believe you are making a mistake.* She pushed them away. He was upset at the time.

She turned to Belle. 'So, I want to hear all the gossip.' Belle had an ear for scandal which enlivened their meetings.

Iris drifted by with a tray, a delicate waft of ash from her pipe coating all the food and drink.

Chapter 8

The following tumultuous months left no time for leisurely gossip at Iris's tea room.

Mr Quoit's Christmas stock had begun to arrive at the warehouse, where it needed to be itemised, sorted, and made ready for display. This involved Clara in hours of dirty, dusty work, aided by Quoit's niece, Jane, who was blessed neither by a pleasing countenance nor an agile intelligence. She was about as much use to Clara as a rickety table. It was arguable that the job would be easier alone, but Quoit insisted that she learn a trade. The dust made Clara cough and then Jane made herself useful by uselessly slapping Clara on the back, which did nothing but make her back ache along with her sore lungs.

When she finished work at the warehouse, she made herself useful to Tom. This took the form of bringing him a pork pie and a pint of ale so he didn't have to stop working, one ill-advised attempt to help paint a doorway (not to be repeated), and sweeping up and generally helping to keep the worksites tidy. It was exhausting after a day's work, but Tom welcomed any help, however small (except the painting).

The main and most material way in which she contributed was in keeping the books in order which was, after all, where she had most experience and talent. For the moment, it was all expenditure on supplies and labour and permits. That was to be expected, but it was disconcerting to say the least to see the loan amount drop day by day by day with nothing yet coming in to balance it. She was used to seeing numbers in both columns. She told herself that this was normal for a new venture. The grand opening of their first premises was the same night as Quoit's big display opening. At that time, she told herself, the other ledger column would start to see the first growth. And as one new shop followed the next, the columns would start to even up until they had the loan amount and interest to repay. It was a good plan, she felt, although, at the end of a busy day, one that would take every bit of their strength. And a huge amount of faith in each other.

And Jacob was working no less hard; Scrooge & Marley was now an actively going concern, which had risen surprisingly quickly for two young men. But Clara knew that neither of them was an ordinary young man. They were driven, in some ways like Tom – in the sense of being ambitious for greater things – but in other ways completely different. Tom had a personal goal, fundamentally driven by his love for Clara and what he wanted for both of them. The business was important, yes, but only for what it could give them. For her brother and Scrooge … it seemed a challenge to make more money than any competitor, not for any specific cause, but just … to have.

Clara mused over this often, when she was sweeping up sawdust or tallying invoices at the end of the day. Ebenezer had, if anything, changed more than Jacob since they joined together, which earned Jacob's hearty approval. And this mattered to Ebenezer. Belle seemed increasingly concerned, on the rare occasions when they were able to talk without interruption.

There were dark smudges under her eyes the last time they met. She seemed even thinner and paler than usual. Her gaze kept straying to the window, as if it held some answer. Since Clara and Tom became customers of the firm, the convivial evenings had stopped. Clara missed these, as did Belle.

'I barely see him now,' said Belle. 'And when I do, it's like he's with someone else. He's always so busy with …'

'Jacob.'

'Yes'. Belle looked directly at her and Clara knew what she was thinking because she had seen it. When she and Tom applied for the loan, Ebenezer had matched his serious countenance almost exactly to Jacob's. It was rather unnerving. Clara considered herself lucky for a moment to be working alongside Tom, even if it was just sweeping up late at night. At least it involved spending time together. Although as fiancé to one of the partners, Belle seemed to be fading somehow.

Clara determined to talk to Jacob about it when they next saw each other, whenever that was.

Two nights later, the opportunity presented itself when Jacob came home a little earlier than usual.

'Oh,' he said, surprised and exhausted. 'I thought you'd be abed by now.'

'Just tidying up a few things.'

He yawned as he hung up his scarf and hat, but she decided to raise the question anyway.

'Jacob, please sit for a minute. I would speak to you about something that concerns both of us.'

'It's late,' he said, but he sat and rubbed his eyes. 'What is it?'

'Not what, but who. Our mutual friend, Ebenezer.' Now she had his attention.

'He is not my friend. Nor yours. He is my partner.'

'I have been talking with Belle. He is neglecting her,

Jacob, which is not how one treats a fiancé. Nor was it in character for him, only a few months ago. You saw how attentive he was and—'

'Clara.' His voice was stern, his eyes cold behind his spectacles. 'This is none of your affair, nor mine.'

She sat back. 'How can you say that?'

'You misunderstand. You always have become personally involved in other people's lives. That is no way to succeed in business. We never discuss any matters other than the firm. Whatever ... dealings he has with Miss Belle are his own.'

'But, Jacob, that is not entirely true, now is it?'

For the first time, he looked uncomfortable.

'You had an opinion of her once, of her being unsuitable because of her lack of dowry and generally low social standing. You thought he could do better.' She remembered the conversation all too well but, at the time, it seemed inconsequential when set against Ebenezer's obvious devotion to Belle. Now it seemed like a prophecy. 'Oh, Jacob ...'

He leaned forward. In the fading candle, Clara noticed the thinning of his hair, the lines of silver at his temples.

'He is my sole partner, so of course I must concern myself with his best interests. If he asks for advice, which he does but rarely, I will give my counsel. I am pleased that he chooses to follow it, but he is in charge of his own destiny, in this and all matters. These are his choices to make.'

'With your influence.'

'It is your choice to see it that way.' He grimaced and rubbed his sternum.

'What is it?'

'Just a bit of indigestion.' He rubbed his chest again. 'This conversation is not helping.' He stood. 'I should think that you and Mr Woodburn had enough of a challenge without taking on someone else's personal problems as well. I suggest you focus on that, and let others run their own affairs.'

And with that, he went into his bedroom and shut the door.

Clara thought over all that Jacob had said. Late as it was, something about his words and demeanour were at odds. Yes, he and Ebenezer's ambitions fed off each other. It was often Ebenezer who saw a way through a tricky transaction. The two of them together were like two sparks of flame, burning brighter in concert. They cared nothing for the opinion of others.

But it went further than that, in a way which eluded her tired mind, some deeper connection between the two of them. Jacob … needed it. He loved Clara, yes, and all the material success was for her comfort, but he needed Ebenezer. There were only tiny glimpses of it, like chinks of light in a brick wall. But it explained a lot of Jacob's decisions: he would put Ebenezer's interests ahead of anyone else's in his partner's life. Anyone's. *How did I not see this before?*

This hint of an insight brought her to full wakefulness. She needed Jacob and Ebenezer too, although for a different reason. She had to trust them. The life planned for her and Tom depended on them.

Life on the street had hardened her too, but differently. Instead of derision and disdain for the poor, she had an impotent yet powerful desire to rescue and redeem: the children, the forgotten detritus of the street. With a focus on the tea shops necessary for the immediate future, this desire most definitely had no place – for now.

And yet she judged people very quickly and with no quarter, which was why Tom was such a revelation. *Oh, Tom.* As soon as her thoughts turned to him, her whole body relaxed. This was the biggest change of all. Without any ruse or other trickery, simply by being good and straight with her, he had won her heart. Completely. Without him trying to own her, she wanted to belong to him. Totally.

She blew out the candle with a heart full of love for him.

And pity for Belle.

As autumn stretched into early winter, the local children started to mingle hopefully by the toy shop window, but she shooed them along with a penny sweet, still weeks to go before the first display. The display coming at the same time as Tom's grand opening was going to stretch even her powers of organisation. But the combined excitement was something she had never experienced before, and she woke to each chilly morning with a feeling of growing anticipation. This would be her most ambitious effort for the shop – and her last – while helping Tom to make a success of his opening. Despite being daunted, she fizzed with energy.

One evening as she shut the warehouse, and was just setting off for Tom's premises, came the first snowflake. She caught it on her tongue. It was a sign. Well, she recognised that as a foolish notion, while choosing to treat it as such all the same. It was early for snow, probably to be followed by rain, but the icy lightness of it on her tongue provided a little festive tingle.

So when Tom came around the corner with Elspeth and the cart, Clara was already smiling.

'A good day?' he asked.

'The first snowflake!'

'Ah, a sign then.'

'I don't believe in signs.'

'Neither do I!' he laughed. He jumped down and lifted her into the cart, heavy with tea chests at the back.

'I was just on my way to see you,' she said.

'We'll get to the shop. First, I want to show you something.'

In the waning afternoon light, he opened the padlock to a wooden shed and lit a lamp. The building stretched back further than was apparent from the lane. The fragrance washed over Clara before she could take in the contents of the shed. It was exotic yet familiar, spicy yet comforting. The smell of the tea transported her, made her feel relaxed, like putting her feet up right on the spot for a cup. And there were chests of it, dozens of them, stacked against the walls. In a few feet of clear floor, Tom had set up a small stove, with two china cups, and a cracked jug of milk.

She scanned the room. 'How much is this stock worth?'

'A fresh shipment from Roderick? I ordered enough for our opening, to be sure it was highest quality, so …'

Clara didn't need an actual figure. She realised they were surrounded essentially by many, many chests full of money. Money waiting to be brewed and drunk.

He poured the tea through a strainer. 'Really,' he said, 'to get the true flavour you should never have milk. That's how they drink it in India. But we have to cater for English tastes. Here, try it.'

She took the cup and drank the clear brown liquid, so different to the murky drink she was used to. The flavour was fresh on her palate, the flavours were far more complex when unveiled: cinnamon and something floral, something earthy with a hint of lemon. Slightly sweet but not cloying. Refreshing, with a hint of tannin in the aftertaste.

'If you can persuade people to try drinking their tea like this,' she said, 'we will make our goal, and maybe more. But even if they carry on as normal, it is an excellent drink.'

With a laugh, he leaned forward to embrace her.

And that was when it happened.

His sleeve caught the edge of the little lamp heating the tea, which toppled off the chest, which ignited some loose straw by his boot, which he stamped on over and over, which only spread the flame across the floor, through the straw, until it reached the first bank of chests where it lapped thirstily at their wooden sides while Tom continued trying to extinguish it until Clara had to haul him by his arm to the door, all the while he tried to batter the flames with his coat.

Tom panting, Clara sobbing, they watched as the air filled with swirling, burning leaves like fiery confetti.

The smell of the burning was revolting, dark and bitter, after the delicious aroma of its brewing.

The elderly carpenter with the next shed got busy dousing his walls. 'I take it the brigade is coming?'

'Yes,' said Tom, faced smeared in soot, 'I'm paid up.' It was one of their first expenses, the brass plaque on the shed that told the fire brigade the subscription had been paid.

'Take some of my water in the meantime,' he said gruffly. 'Could be a while.'

Paying the fee was no guarantee of promptness, and so it turned out. The smoke-filled air brought on Clara's cough and she had to retreat to recover herself. From a distance, she watched as Tom, the old carpenter and half a dozen others ran in and out with pails of water, but only succeeded in soaking whatever didn't burn.

It smelled of death: the death of a dream.

The fire brigade arrived just as the last flame was doused. The whole stinking mess smouldered in the grey light of dawn. With a lot of rueful head-shaking, the others packed up their buckets and went home for an hour's sleep before the working day.

Tom slumped beneath the dripping remains of the roof, head in his hands, Clara beside him.

'It was not your—' she began.

'Stop, Clara. Just stop.'

'I will talk to Jacob—'

'Please. Stop.' He turned to her. 'This is my responsibility.' His eyes were red from smoke, rimmed black with soot, and shadowed with exhaustion. 'We are ruined. I have ruined us. Oh, Clara …'

'This is *our* responsibility. We are not ruined. Not yet, anyway. We need a plan.' Despite her effort at calm, her mind whirled at the damage and could not yet take in the size and scale of the calamity facing them. She clutched her hands together to stop them shaking, but Tom turned to her.

'All right then,' he said. 'We owe the money, whatever all this sets us back. Which is a lot, I can tell you. I can't see … I can't see a way through. But there must be one.'

She pulled him to his feet. 'Neither can I, at the moment. We need food and rest and thought. There must be ways we can cut back, ways we can do with less. I will go through every line. We will make it work, somehow.' She had no idea where this confidence came from, except necessity. 'We need a plan. Tomorrow, Tom. We will come up with a plan tomorrow.'

He wrapped her in his arms. She laid her head on his shoulder.

'I love you, Clara Belle Marley,' he said in her ear.

'I love you too. That is why we will find a way.'

Chapter 9

The table was strewn with estimates, demands for payments, drawings and contracts. Motes danced in the bright sunshine, as if to mock their downfall. On his way out of the door that morning, Jacob had taken both her shoulders in a strong embrace and said, 'I am sorry this has happened.' And he kissed her cheek and was gone.

'One shop,' said Tom.

They had been over the figures and facts four times this morning so far, drinking the tea strong and bitter.

'One shop,' agreed Clara. 'The best, most welcoming, well equipped we can make it. It will be so inviting that, before long, we will have the custom to expand. It might not have to be another shop, there is potential to add more space to the one you have.'

Tom leaned back and stared at his hands. 'It is a start.' He raised his eyes. 'But you also understand the problem that we face with one shop, no matter how inviting.'

Clara nodded. There was no point in talking of expansion. Their ability to maintain the loan payments – and repay it all ultimately – had receded further from them with each burning tea chest. One shop could never generate enough profit. 'There's only one thing to do: we must proceed with the grand opening and use the success to persuade Ebenezer and Jacob that the plan is still sound. It is a reasonable approach.'

'You know your brother.'

Yes, she thought, *I do. But I have also seen the queue of debtors who have fallen behind: the women in tears, the men in stoic despair as they are shown the door. That he is my brother, that must count for something. Surely?* Even more so, their proposition meant that Scrooge & Marley would recoup more of their investment. This, she knew, would count heavily in their favour.

'And Roderick can get us enough in time for the opening?'

'Yes, if I order today, he will get it here. He is a good bloke, you would like him.'

'That is something.'

They looked at the table between them. On it, Clara pictured a pair of clockwork figurines, like in part of her display for the shop: there they were, dancing a wedding waltz, then swinging a dark-haired toddler in a laughing arc, then walking the path to a cottage with a puffing chimney … all bathed in a golden glow of warmth and togetherness. She felt not only a fierce desire to live it, but an equally fierce desire to protect it.

'What do you see?' he asked.

'Happiness.' The scene dissolved against the bare wood. 'Our happiness.'

Tom's face was clouded with worry, the great brows bunched together like a stormy sky. She saw everything wrapped up there – his hopes, his fears, his determination and oh, so much pride, all tied together by his love for her.

She smoothed his cheek and his eyes cleared. 'We have a chance, just one. Most people do not get that.'

'Well then, Miss Marley,' and he kissed the palm of her hand.

'Mr Woodburn.'

'We shall take it.'

And they went out into the sparkling chill of the morning.

Later that afternoon, as the light was leaving the sky, came a quiet knock at the shop: the one Clara was dreading.

Belle stood on the other side of the glass, with only a thin cardigan around her shoulders.

Clara put on her jacket and called, 'Tom, I will be back.'

Belle was even thinner than before, delicate bones covered by the palest of skin, beautiful but as ephemeral as a raindrop. Clara bundled her into the fug of Iris's tea room, sat her down and ordered two slabs of cake, coffee and cream.

Belle's eyes were dry but red. 'It is over. I have ended it.'

Clara took her hands as the cake and coffee arrived. 'Tell me what happened.'

Belle shrugged. 'Nothing dramatic. Just indifference on top of uncaring. Not cruel, just … absent. He never looked directly at me, as if I was not really there.' She turned confused eyes on Clara. 'Maybe that is cruel? What do you think?'

It was not exactly cruel, but just the opposite of kind.

'I felt like I was haunting him. So,' Belle continued, 'I released him. I could not continue to feel like a ghost in his life, unseen and unwanted.'

'I am so, so sorry.'

'And yet not shocked, or even surprised, my dear friend. You have noticed the changes in him too since … since …'

Clara struggled to hold's Belle's gaze, and not turn away from the intense pain there, as Ebenezer had done. Honesty was the very least she owed. 'Yes, I have, since the business began taking up so much time for both of them.'

'But it is more than that, and I know you see it too.' A little colour appeared in Belle's cheeks, like fever spots. 'Ebenezer was not like this before, you saw for yourself. He wanted success, of course, but he had interest in other things ... other people.' She shook her head and removed a handkerchief from her sleeve. 'No more. I know Jacob never thought I was good enough for him, but even so ...'

Clara could not contradict her, but was struck by how casually Jacob had contributed to this chain of events. He would simply see it as the resolution to a rather awkward and inconvenient situation – not the ruination of someone's happiness. *Marriage is a business transaction*, he had said, *an exchange of goods and services*.

Clara knew him so well, yet a part of her heart hardened towards him. 'What will you do?'

'I have an aunt in Shropshire, blind, who needs a companion. It's a sweet little place, I spent a few summers there.' She looked around. 'I will miss you, Clara, but I will not miss London. No, not at all.' And with that, she rose and left. Clara's eyes stayed on her until she disappeared into the crowd.

Two months later, and London shone her festive face. The shops were full, and smartly dressed livery men transported gay parcels and packages in gleaming black carriages. Food and drink, and more food and drink, were loaded on barrows and shoulders and carts, shivering ponies steaming the air with their breath. There were whistles and bagpipes and the always mournful-sounding charity brass band, and even a string quartet outside the fruiterer's. The raw bloody waft of the butcher's shop was softened by the sweet buttery smell of pastry from the baker's, everything spiced by the bowers of greenery gracing the doorways and corners.

And while work continued inside Tom's Teas, a boy ladled hot, fragrant tea to passers-by outside, all the while calling, 'Grand Opening in one week! You don't want to miss it!'

Clara tucked her hair into her bonnet although she was very warm from her exertions at the toy shop. She and Jane had been at work through the night, stacking and arranging, decorating and creating tableaux which brought out the inner nature of each toy and showed it off to its best advantage.

She stood back from the shop window to admire her efforts, and was rewarded by the pushing, shoving gallery of children ranged in front of the big bay window. Grubby hands and fists at the glass, little mouths hanging open in wonderment, all awash with the gilded light flooding over them. The smallest children struggled to get a view of anything but others' backs.

Clara retrieved her penny sweets, brought for this purpose. She clapped her gloved hands but few heads turned, so engrossed were they in choosing exactly the right thing, if that opportunity ever came along in their short lives. 'Children, there is space for everyone to have a good look, just be polite and don't push. And here—' She tossed a large handful of sweets into the air, which made small indentations where they landed in the slush.

Now there was a scrabble for the sweets, she marshalled several smaller viewers into place. 'There you go,' she said, patting heads. There were some who reminded her of the young Jacob, one boy in particular that could not help but stare until he looked away with a distrustful glance and scuttled off. Everyone knew of the gangs who roamed looking to scoop up the street children and put them to work – what kind of work was not spoken of, but somehow the warnings got around.

Four times, she reorganised her display, until she felt satisfied that the customers were as well. Her piles of boxes, skeins of ribbon, and jars of glitter were all depleted. Mr Quoit stood by the front door, greeting customers, hands crossed over his ample frontage.

'Good use of space, Miss Marley. Good use of colour. I am pleased with this.' He nodded. 'Yes, I am pleased with it. And good to see Jane involved.'

Jane had mostly spent the night curled up in a packing crate, but some of the ideas were hers.

The shop was lit up with the whole spectrum of golden light, from treacly dark yellow along the bottom margin silhouetting its heaving, jostling sticky-nosed gaggle, up through the paler yellows of a sunny summer day. Clara paused to reflect, 'Can it really be another Christmas already?'

She lingered to capture her reflection in one of the dimpled glass panels, and was instantly taken back to those days, in her torn and ragged dress, her hair matted and dirty, her skin blotchy with sores. She turned away from the reflection, scattering sweets in all directions. *No. Those days are gone.* A cold wind whistled down the street, so chill it took her breath away. She coughed in reply, her throat feeling constricted. It passed, but she coughed again soon after. And again. Some of the waifs glanced away from the window, drawn by the sound of the nice lady with the sweets coughing and coughing. Mr Quoit appeared at his door and put his arm about her shoulder.

'Come in from the cold,' he said soothingly. 'Should you not purchase something for that cough?'

Clara had recovered now and said simply, 'It has always been with me, that is, since I was a child of a certain age. It is nothing.' *Those days are gone*, she thought again. *But some things remain. Time does not heal everything.*

Chapter 10

Three months had passed since the grand opening of Tom's first tea shop. Custom had been steady but not spectacular. And what they had needed, Tom and Clara, was something spectacular. It was a cold March morning when Clara welcomed Tom through her front door. His face had the look of storm clouds gathering, his eyes dark-ringed with worry and the wrinkles around his eyes that crinkled with laughter served only to accentuate his fatigue.

'Do not fret, dear Tom,' said Clara, straightening his cravat and forcing herself to smile. 'It is my brother we are meeting after all, not a stranger. Not a hard-hearted banker who does not know us from Adam.'

'No,' Tom grimaced. 'But a hard-hearted brother instead.'

Clara was taken a little aback by this, but tried not to show it. She felt defensive of her brother, yet knew that Tom spoke the truth, mostly.

'He was not always thus,' she said quietly.

Tom apologised and smiled painfully at her. He fetched her cloak and hat from where she'd placed them ready on the hall table.

'Tie it snug, for there is an east wind blowing outside,' said Tom. 'And I never did like an east wind.'

Together they walked slowly to the office of Scrooge & Marley. London was rising from its winter days amid hints of spring: greening buds had appeared on the plane trees, sweet violets crept along quiet paths and under hedgerows, daffodils trumpeted their brand of sunshine from indoor vases. It was a time of renewal and beginnings, but for these two walkers it felt like they proceeded towards an ending, a closing down. They did not speak as they walked, their only communication being periodic squeezes of Clara's hands about Tom's broad forearm. Too soon, they reached their destination, and entered.

The meeting began formally, with Ebenezer and Jacob seated on one side of the desk and Tom and Clara opposite them. Between them lay a hillock of papers, bills, receipts and demands, all related to Tom's Teas. Ebenezer had been talking through them, highlighting the poor investment they represented, all spoken in a flat tone with a flat face. Jacob stared grimly ahead or at the desk. Not once did he look at his sister or her beau, though Clara gazed at him throughout, willing him to meet her eye.

Scrooge finished his examination with a final question: 'I understand you have family in Scotland. Is it not possible for any of them to lend you the money to pay off your debts?'

Tom looked down and said quietly, 'It is not. None of my close family have the necessary capital.'

'I thought as much,' said Jacob, with a look of distaste. *So, you speak at last,* thought Clara, *and still you cannot look at me.* He continued, 'Therefore, it behoves me to conclude that the business has not been a success and will never be one, indeed not fast enough to pay off all of these debts. It is a failure and thus must be ended as soon as manageable, in order to recoup losses swiftly. Scrooge & Marley hereby give notice, with immediate effect, on calling in our loan.'

Clara gasped but Tom was silent. 'Please, Jacob...' she began.

But Jacob was shaking his head, still refusing to look at her. 'And this is why I advised that you should not be present, my dear. As I am not Jacob here and this is not Ebenezer. We are Scrooge & Marley and this is business.'

'Understood,' Tom said gruffly and pushed his chair back with a harsh scrape, and stood.

'But we are four people who …' Clara continued, not willing to give up the ghost quite yet.

'We are nothing here but two sides of a transaction,' interrupted Jacob, his voice sharper than before.

Tom shuffled his large feet awkwardly and said, 'I will need to write to my cousin in India as regards finances. Will you give me leave to hear back from him before proceeding?'

'No, we will not give you leave to wait for correspondence from such a place,' said Scrooge.

'Ebenezer!' cried Clara. Her throat felt constricted. She knew these two would be tough nuts to crack, but their coldness was like an icy hand about her neck.

'Again, dear sister,' said Jacob with mock patience, 'do not allow yourself to mix business with prior associations. Now then, Woodburn, you must close the business immediately. You must sell off remaining stock and equipment immediately. Of course, write to your cousin if you will, but there will be no waiting period. All assets must be sold and the profits gained handed to us.'

Clara had rehearsed a little speech over and over the night before, about the prospects for Tom's Teas and the customers that had become regulars. She planned to tell them of the praise of local dignitaries such as the doctor's wife who always took her tea with lemon, the nephew of an opera singer who came each day for his strong black cup and an antiques dealer who had once sourced candlesticks for the Lord Mayor's uncle, who said that the quality of the brew was 'exceedingly fine'. But Clara did not have the chance to tell her stories, as Tom was already at the door and her brother and his partner were tidying away the papers with their mouths set in hard arches.

Tom opened the door and held it open for Clara to come through, clearly desperate to escape the place. Clara stood reluctantly, gave one last look about, to which nobody responded, and stepped out into the street, whereupon the east wind blasted them both in the face and she nearly lost her bonnet. Her eyes stung with the street dust whipped up by the gust, but they then filled with tears from the shock and humiliation of the mere fifteen minutes they had spent in the office of Scrooge & Marley, fifteen minutes that had changed her life for ever.

She remembered what Jacob had said to her about taking over Fezziwig's business. *It's nothing personal. Just business.* Well, now was not the time or the place to do so, but tonight, when they warmed their feet by the fire after dinner, she would speak to her brother and she would make it personal.

'I will speak to him, Tom,' she said loudly as they

walked into the buffeting breeze. Spots of chilled rain were flung at their cheeks, making conversation a trial. But she simply must speak with Tom, who was ploughing on relentlessly, forcing her to almost run to keep up with him. He did not reply. 'I will make him see, don't worry.'

Tom suddenly stopped, almost causing her to trip over his boots. She looked up and realised they were close to her home. The rain was coming down on them now, the wind flinging wet handfuls at them like a taunt. 'Clara, my dear, you will not speak to your brother of this. This is between myself and the office of Scrooge & Marley. It is a matter for men and so it will stay.'

He would not look in her eye, instead holding on to his hat to save it from the bullying wind, he stared off up the street in the direction he must walk back to his shop.

'Tom, my dearest, you have never spoken to me thus. I can see that you are—'

But he would not let her finish. 'And while we're about it, I release you from any understanding you may have had with me. Now I am bankrupt I cannot marry. I am no good to you nor to anyone else. Now I must go, for I have a hundred sickening tasks awaiting me. Goodbye, Miss Marley.'

And off he went, swallowed by the boiling crowds of London. The skies tipped great buckets of rain upon them all, the water sheeting in freezing grey veils that soaked her through. She watched her future stride away from her, as she stood alone outside the house she shared with Jacob Marley of Scrooge & Marley, for she could not call it a home, not now. Her throat seized with a convulsion and she began to cough. She coughed and coughed, bending over in the street, ignored by busy passers-by. She tried to drag herself up the steps to her front door, but was coughing too hard to manage it. She sank down in the rain and knocked weakly on the broad hardwood, that would not open. She fought to control her breathing, though her throat was wracked with pain and her ribs with jarring shivers. She had never felt so alone, as she believed in that moment that she was bereaved of everything: her husband-to-be, her hopes and dreams, her health, her home, and her brother. All was lost.

That evening, Jacob sat beside her sickbed and would not leave her. She slept fitfully, woken often by her coughing and the shivers, her sleep full of nightmares of great piles of tea leaves and bank notes burning acridly, choking her, the embers floating on the warm draughts and singeing her face and hands as she fought to swipe them away. But then another dream came, a pleasant place not of the heat of flames, but of the heat of the sun, warming her very bones, surrounding her with health and life. She could smell the scent of exotic tea leaves wafting to her and hear the chirping of unfamiliar birds. In her dream, she was in a foreign land. She saw Tom standing beside a field of tea plants, in white shirt-sleeves and pale brown trousers, his skin bronzed by the climate. Beyond him a man in a broad-brimmed hat was writing figures in a great book, his face turned away so she could not see him. But she knew, in the way we do in dreams, that this was Tom's cousin, Roderick. The warm breeze ruffled her face but she knew she was not there, she was only an observer, she knew that Tom and anyone else could not see her. But she possessed the knowledge that this dream told the future, Tom's future, the answer to all of their earthly problems.

At the quietest hour of the night she awoke, the candle guttering on the shelf, Jacob slumped over in his chair. They had not spoken of the meeting, as she had not had the wherewithal to discuss anything from earlier that day. His presence was appreciated by Clara but left a bitter aftertaste. She watched him grumble in his chair-bound sleep and resented the brotherly affection shown in his bedside vigil. Why could he not have shown such regard in his dealings with her fiancé?

'Jacob,' she said, which set off a cough and made him stir. 'Jacob,' she managed again and he awoke with a start, leaning towards her.

'All is well, my dear. The doctor said it is but a chill. You will rally. Rest, Clara.'

'Listen,' she whispered, as not voicing her words was less likely to set off another fit. 'Call for Tom. I wish to see Tom.'

'At this hour?' cried Jacob. 'You are not yourself. It is the small hours of the morning.'

'In daylight then. I beg of you. Call for Tom. I wish to see him.'

'Yes, my dear. When the day comes.'

'Promise me,' she muttered.

'I promise. Now, sleep. Tomorrow will be better.'

She allowed her heavy eyelids to droop, her brother's face sharp then hazy, sharp again, then gone. She dreamt of him as the boy Jake, the hard-edged face at the toy shop window, his thin arms about her on the streets, the words he spoke to her every night: *I promise that we will have a good life again. And I will always keep you safe.*

When she awoke in the thin light of a grey morning, her dreams had told her a truth she had forgotten:

that her brother wanted her with him always, that he had moved heaven and earth to keep them alive and keep them together. In her love for Tom, she had forgotten this, but it did not make it right. Wanting to marry, to move on into her own life and make her own family, were wholly natural desires. But Jake showed none of these instincts. Business had become his life, his family playing second fiddle. She remembered that as a child, after the bad times had come for them, more than anything, she wanted to be part of a family again. But Jake's more-than-anything was not the same as hers; his desire was never to be poor again. As she lay wheezing in her bed, listening to her brother taking his daily wash in the next room, she realised that the harsh life they had led on the streets had sent them off in opposing directions: it had turned her towards pity and love, it had turned him towards hardness and avarice. How could she possibly change his path now? She knew it would be hard, if not impossible, yet she also knew that if anyone could change Jacob Marley, his beloved sister would be the only one who could.

Jacob was true to his midnight promise and Tom arrived mid-morning, once she was breakfasted on a thin gruel that gave her a little sustenance, and was propped up in bed. Her cough was still there, but not as violent as the day before and her fever had cooled somewhat, though she still felt very weak. Tom came in, cap in hand, seeming far too large for the room and the chair he was given to sit on. But his face was the very picture of loving concern, with a hint of shame about his tired eyes.

'Do not speak, dear Clara,' he said softly. 'I can see you are too weak for conversation. I received a message from your brother that you were ill and wished to see me. But he told me at the door that I must not stay more than a minute and I concur. So, here I am and here I must leave you. You must rest, my dear, and get well again.'

'No,' she whispered, holding her breath for a moment until the desire to cough had passed. 'I must speak with you.'

'But, my dear—'

'Listen to me,' she insisted, quiet but forthright. 'I will wait for you. However long it takes for you to find your feet, I will wait.'

Tom looked at his feet and shook his head. 'I cannot allow that,' he said sadly. 'It will not do.' She reached out her hand and Tom looked up at her, taking it so gently, so tenderly, it brought a tear to her eye. She struggled to speak but she knew these were words that must be said now, at this moment. 'It will do and you will allow it. I am yours and you are mine. We shall weather this brief storm. If you deny me, you will break my heart.'

Tom's eyes too had filled with tears, one brimming over and rolling down his round cheek, swiftly followed by another. 'I could never knowingly bring you pain, my love.'

'Then do this for me. Tell my brother you will go to India. You will work for your cousin Roderick. You will send a portion of your earnings to my brother until a certain percentage of the debt is paid off. I will agree the percentage with him. When the percentage is reached, you will come home and we shall marry. I will arrange this with Jacob. He will do this small thing for me. But for you, it is a considerable thing. To sail abroad, to work hard in the sun. But I fear it is the only way, and the alternative I fear more: that of debtors' prison. But this way, you will work your way out of debt and secure our future. What do you say, Tom?'

The immense effort it took to make this speech immediately took its toll and the cough she had held back to achieve it came upon her like a tidal wave, crippling her body so that she thought she would die from it. She could hear Tom's terrified voice call for help but after that she heard nothing, as she passed out from exhaustion.

*

The days after passed in confusion. She did not see Tom again – only in her dreams, but not in the waking world – and she was tended by a pale face she did not know, the uniform signalling a hired nurse, who had a kind voice and cool hands. It was many moons before she came out of the fever and could see straight, let alone think straight. She remembered that the day after she had fallen ill, Tom had come to her and she had told him of her plan. She hoped it was real and not merely an imagining induced by her illness. One morning, sitting up in bed drinking broth, she felt well enough to call for her brother and discuss the matter that was burning in the forefront of her mind. Jacob confirmed that Tom had been to see him, that they had come to an arrangement, that he would work off the debt in India, then come home to England when it was paid.

'I hoped there would be an understanding that a percentage could be paid off, not the entire debt.'

'No, my dear,' said Jacob. 'We agreed on the entire debt.'

She had not the energy in her to argue with him, but decided this was a conversation that could be had in the near future after Tom had gone. She could work on her brother's resolve between now and then, she had faith. 'Will you send for Tom, so that we can discuss his travel arrangements?'

'Oh, but his ship has already sailed. He has gone to India. We agreed there was no need to wait, that the sooner he set off, the sooner he would begin to pay off his debt. He will be en route as we speak, six days in to a month's journey or more, I should think.'

Clara was shocked by the news and saddened she would not see her Tom's face for a long time, that they had not discussed it further, that he had not said good-bye. But she was proud of him too, for acting in such a forthright manner and taking charge of their future so resolutely. She regretted his absence but admired his resolve.

'I am sure he will write to you, my dear. Until then, rest assured that I will be here to look after your needs. As I always have been and as I always will be.'

Chapter 11

A hundred days had passed since Tom's ship had left England. Clara had spent many of these in bed, recuperating. The doctor told her that her cough was a symptom of a deeper ill, a weakness in her lungs made worse by the rigours her poor little body suffered on the streets, all those years before. It had weakened her heart also and thus she must live a quiet life thereon in, with no cause for over-excitement or over-exertion. She would have to give up her employment at the toy shop, of course, yet Jacob assured her that the business was doing so well that she need have no fear over finances. She must simply rest and build up her strength again. This was welcome news of course, that their household economy was safe despite her illness, but it was tinged with resentment, that it was most likely due to the suffering of nameless others that her brother's business was succeeding, others like Tom who had fallen foul of the money-lending partners, Scrooge and Marley.

Summer came and went, the warm weather like a distant dream to Clara, as she ventured out little and mostly stayed in the house, reading. Her brother was always happy to see her seated with a book. It seemed to soothe him, that she was resting, that her mind was employed usefully. The books she had sent to her from the bookseller were a variety of titles, from novels to treatises on domestic harmony, from histories of fallen empires to pretty verses. But there were some books she kept hidden from her brother and only took out when she was quite sure he was gone from the house: books about the science of tea growing and of life in the exotic and far-flung country of India. For Clara was formulating her own plan. The moment she had word from Tom, she was going to write back to him and suggest she come to him. She felt so much better than she had for months. Her lungs were still somewhat fragile, but she was convinced that the hot weather in India would be good for her, would be healthful and revitalising. Cold lay cruelly on a person's weak chest, the kind of creeping, sneaking cold of a London winter, hung heavy with fog and choking vapours. She could not bear to spend another Christmas in England without her husband-to-be. She asked the servants day in, day out, if word had come, if a letter had arrived from India, if there was anything from Mr Woodburn. Then, one early September day, it came.

Thankfully, Jacob was at the office and she could indulge in the wonder of it alone. She decided to postpone the glory of it by taking a short walk. The streets were still cloaked in summer greens, the flower-sellers – rain-soaked in spring but now basking in sunshine – handed out dahlias and lilies; the greengrocers' punnets were loaded with English berries, wasps lazily bothering the heaped piles of jewelled fruits. She held the letter to her heart and walked swiftly towards her favourite square, one that contained a small garden and benches to sit on and watch the weary world go by. She could not help but smile, her face upturned to the sun, drawing goodness and light from it, imagining the same sun shining down on her beloved Tom on the other side of the earth. *Soon*, she thought, *my dear. Soon.*

She seated herself on a bench and took out the letter. It was a miracle, to see her name scrawled across the small, battered envelope that had crossed land and sea to sit neatly now in her hands. There was a moment where she thought the handwriting was unfamiliar, that it did not seem reminiscent of

Tom's. But as she turned it over to open it, she recalled that it was many months since she had seen Tom's handwriting and perhaps she had forgotten its likeness. Inside were two letters, one on fine, thick paper, the other enclosed in its own sealed envelope, very crumpled and forlorn, with another's hand having written her name and address on its front. Was this Tom's handwriting? She could not be sure, but a chill ran up her spine and she placed that letter on the bench beside her and hurriedly opened the letter on the finer paper first.

Dear Miss Marley,

My name is Roderick Fairleigh and I am the cousin of Mr Tom Woodburn. He was coming to India to work with me at managing our tea plantations. I believe that you were a person who was acquainted with my cousin, as I have found a letter to you among his effects. I have enclosed this letter, which was written on board ship. It is with great sadness that I must inform you that my cousin did not reach these shores, as he took a bad case of fever during his journey and he passed away at sea. My servant was given his effects upon the ship's arrival, including the letter addressed to yourself. I understand that his body was buried at sea, as is ship's custom. As you can see, I did not

open the sealed letter to yourself, thus I am still unaware of
the nature of your acquaintanceship with Mr Woodburn.
I would be happy to hear from you if you would like to
correspond with me further, yet I do not have any further
information for you at this time. I regret having to write
this kind of news to any person and hope you will forgive
any indelicacy on my part in the conveying of this most
tragic of announcements. I am adept at handling the leaves
of tea, but not of paper, I am ashamed to say. Suffice to say,
my cousin Tom was a good man from a good family and
will be missed. I have written to his family to inform them
of his passing.

Yours sincerely,
Roderick Fairleigh Esq.

He is dead. Tom is dead. A dense, final voice in her mind
spoke the words as clear as day.

Clara's hand reached clumsily down for the sealed
envelope beside her, a sudden terror that she did not
have it in her hand and it was the very last vestige of
Tom she would ever touch and see. She went to tear
it open but stopped, her hands trembling, aware that
this was the most treasured object she had ever held
in her grasp. She turned it over and began to inch her
way along the seal with infinite care, lest she damage

the precious contents in any small way. She retrieved the letter. It was written on coarse paper, smudged with yellow and brown stains. The hand was spidery, punctuated by many black blots of ink, evidence of a shaky grip on the pen that wrote it. To see Tom's likeness in his handwriting, to think of the figures she had seen him write on his tea shop's papers, to think of all that was lost, these thoughts came over her like a black wave of hot tea, threatening to scald and drown her. She closed her eyes to steady herself, but this made her head swim, so she forced herself to open them and focus her gaze on the letter before her, sitting so innocently in her lap.

My dearest Clara,

I write this with a shaking hand. I am in a bad way. A fever has gripped me and I am fearful. The ship's surgeon is not hopeful. I wanted to write before I became too weak. If I am to never see land, I have to tell you that I adored you, dear heart, more than anything. I want you to know that I will leave this earth with no incomplete business, as my life was made complete by meeting you and knowing that you loved me. I can go to my maker with a light heart and will wait to see you again in that better place. But I hope not to meet you there soon, for I wish you to live a long and

fruitful life, to find love elsewhere. I hope you leave your
brother and seek a life for yourself beyond his walls. That
sounds bitter and I am sorry for that, but I do want you
to be free, my love, truly free. My only regret is that I was
not the one to welcome you to that life of freedom. Please
forgive me, for my many failures. Please know that I loved
you always. You are my angel.

Yours,
Tom

Clara Belle Marley stood up from the bench and began to walk. It was as if her body had been entered by a spirit that did the walking for her. She felt as if she were floating above her life, no longer a part of it. She walked and she walked, through the streets of London, surrounded by the bright spirits of humanity – the pedlars, the hawkers, the vendors, the dealers; the whelk-sellers and waggoners, the needlewomen and boardmen, the sweeps and the shoe-blacks; the road-menders and locksmiths, the recruiting sergeants and linen-draper's assistants; the oakum-pickers and stone-breakers, the mudlarks and crawlers, the idlers and vagabonds. From bottom to top, the wretches, the workers, the shabby-genteel and the gentle folk: every hue of social class in the great dirty rainbow of the city. She had the sensation of thousands of alert minds wholly cut off from each other, each one assured of its own importance in its own story of its own life. London was a monstrous kaleidoscope of isolated bodies, negotiating the chaotic jumbling paths of others as do boiling peas in a pot. She saw that the trick of life was to stop, to reach out, to connect. It was the next best thing to mind-reading: loving someone. But love came at a price and that was loss. Was it not better to stay a hermit of the soul, to live within one's self and never venture forth? A multitude of souls swarmed about her like a bubbling spring of life and she felt that she was not a part of it any more. Her body, so weakened by her illness before this, seemed to derive a power of perambulation from beyond herself, the two feet driving forwards. Her mind followed, vacant, seeing only but not thinking. For thinking was too hard, too upsetting and too real. She had divorced herself from life, as life had struck her the cruellest blow.

Her feet, by way of a circuitous route only they seemed to fathom, brought her back full circle to Percy Street. She passed by the old toy shop where she had stood as a ragamuffin and worked as a woman. She could not look opposite to the site of Tom's business. She could not turn her head to see it. Her feet went onwards. They took her west, up street and down alley, until at last they stopped. A sign hung stiffly in the late afternoon sun, proclaiming the business's name: Scrooge & Marley. A bell tinkled as she walked in, her mind thrown back to her visit there with Tom some months before. This sad remembrance only strengthened her resolve. She walked past a gawping assistant, past Ebenezer saying something to her, standing up and moving towards her, until she reached Jacob's room and entered without knocking, to find him alone at his desk, scratching his damnable numbers in a ledger. He looked up, shocked, and was about to address her when her mouth opened and out came words, though she had no control over what issued and she felt quite keenly that she was standing outside herself watching the scene unfold.

'He is dead,' she said.

'My dear, what on earth …?'

'Tom is dead. I have the letter here. He died of a fever on board ship.'

Jacob stood and came around the desk, reached out to touch her arm, but she stepped back firmly, almost stumbling over a hat-stand behind her. She squared up to him and he looked somewhat alarmed.

'Clara, come home with me.'

'No, I will not. You will hear me. It is my fault Tom is dead.'

'It is nothing of the sort. If he died aboard ship, it is providence, bad luck. It is the way of the world. These things happen, tragic as they are.'

'No. You are wrong. I suggested he go. It was my idea. I am to blame.'

Jacob shook his head and replied, 'No, Clara, that is not the case. Tom had had the same idea as you before you suggested it to him. He told me so when we discussed it during your illness. It was his choice to go to India. And what other choice did he have in any case? The singular alternative was the shame of languishing in prison with the other debtors.'

'You are right,' said Clara. 'The fault does not lie with me. Or with Tom. It lies with you. If you had helped us in our hour of need, instead of treating us like debt-ridden blackguards rather than your beloveds.'

'Ha!' Jacob scoffed. 'Tom Woodburn was not my beloved! He was simply a bad businessman. And never good enough for a sister of mine, if truth be told.'

'You would speak ill of the dead? Within minutes of hearing of his passing?'

'If I am challenged upon his usefulness, yes.'

'He was my life!'

'Come now, Clara. Do pull yourself together. You

are a Marley and we are strong. We have survived and overcome losses worse than this. Our dear parents, remember? I did not protect you on the streets all those years to have you pine away over a romance like a love-struck kitchen maid.'

Her strength had been growing as she had spoken to him, as her rage grew mightier. At this moment, she found she was not standing outside herself any longer and instead was fully present, looking through her own eyes at this hard-edged human being she had once loved more than any other person on earth.

'You have no heart. You have no soul. You are made of ice, of stone, of wood, of hard substance with no give, no curve, no bend. No warmth or life. When we were children, and the rich stepped over the poor on the street, you sought revenge. But you are no better. You are worse, because you know how the poor suffer and you take your riches from it. You inhale the life from others like an evil spirit and feast upon their suffering.'

Jacob looked upon her with a cold eye. He seemed without retort for a moment, or perhaps he was weighing up his words. Then, he spoke: 'I have no regrets and I never will. I did everything I could to help us survive, but even this was not enough, as your cough that started in the workhouse is a symptom of the poverty that is ailing you now. Poverty will always be with us, in our very blood and bones. But it will not vanquish me. I swore to you that we will never be poor again. And I have made good on my promise. And, now, you dare to attack me for it? You, a sickly spinster, with no prospects? I am all you have left. You would do well to remember that, seeing as your very livelihood depends on me. So, you will have to swallow your disgust and loathing of the way I put bread and meat on your table and you will have to curb your tongue, unless it is to thank me.'

If she had been capable of witchcraft, she might have cursed him. She felt a hatred flowing through her, which sickened and exhausted her. She mustered what little strength she had left and simply said, 'Jacob Marley, you will regret it if you do not change your ways.'

As she sought for more words to hurl at him, a wave of fatigue overcame her and she put her hand to her head, swaying dangerously to one side.

Jacob took hold of her arms and said more softly, wheedling now, 'You must not upset yourself like this, sister. You have had bad news, that is all. Here, let me take you home. Everything will seem better once your health improves. I will pay for a new doctor to see you, a superior one. Let us take you to rest now. You know not what you are saying. We have both said too much. But do not fret, as I forgive you for your outburst. I forgive you.'

Clara closed her eyes as the faintness took her. She could not speak them aloud, but inside her head the bitter words rang out, hollow like a death knell: *But I do not forgive you.*

PART III: THE END

Chapter 12

Over the ensuing months, Clara's body underwent a transformation. In the space of a fortnight, weight dropped from her and her cheeks became gaunt. At first, she asked for a hand mirror to see her changing face for herself – her eyes peered out at her as dark caves – but she soon discarded it as the truth of her condition became too woeful to witness. She did not want to eat or to move from her bed. Jacob was at his wits' end, striding up and down in the next room. Between her persistent fits of coughing, in the rare moments of stillness, her brow damp from night sweats, she would hear his footsteps tramping to and fro, to and fro, a pacing litany to her thoughts. She thought much of Tom, of course, of his final days, but also of their time together. She tortured herself with thoughts of how – if he had stayed, if the tea had not burnt, if they had married, if Scrooge & Marley had not called in the loan – her body might be transforming in another way these days, a natural, beautiful change, ripening into motherhood. Now, it was shrinking towards nothingness.

It was seven days before Christmas Eve. Her entire existence was reduced to the fight for breath. Her thoughts strayed rarely from the constant, urgent need to draw air into her damaged lungs and expel it again, without triggering the crippling, blood-speckled cough, her constant companion. Jacob did not leave her bedside that day. He spoke little. There was so little to say. He placed his cold, bony hand upon hers from time to time. He looked into her eyes with a kind of searching fever, then looked away. She could not help him now and this saddened her. It was so hard to speak but she wanted to say something of comfort to him. But every word was a combat with the consumption and she had not the vitality left for anything but breath, breath, breath. The day grew dark and night cloaked her chamber in the hue of ink and crows, of priests and doctors. Jacob lit a solitary candle, which threw queer shadows upon the wall, flickering strange companions to his vigil. She wanted only to speak three words to him. She mouthed them several times before any sound could issue. His head had been down, lost in his own miserable thoughts. As he looked up, he saw her lips moving and leaned in close.

'What is it, my dear, my love?' His voice was high, breathy, reminiscent of his boyhood tones.

'I … forgive … you,' she said, every word a prodigious effort, every word a burden falling from her poor, wracked form, leaving her lightened and free, ready to depart.

Jacob wept, loudly and long. The clock on the mantelpiece rang out the chimes for midnight and before the twelfth bell had sounded, Clara Belle Marley was dead.

The days following were shrouded in heavy fog, a true London particular that made the outside world seem fantastical to Jacob. He dealt with the deeds that needed to be done following the passing of one human into the next world; he was good at such things, arrangements, paperwork, bills and so forth. He was not good at feeling, at longing, at regretting or grieving. His brain was forged from figures, quills, pen-knives and papers, with no gaps for the softer things of life, of matters of the heart. His sister had suffered from consumption and she had died. Business went on, debtors went on, money went on, life went on. After her body had been removed to the funeral home, he drew the curtains about her bed himself, then instructed a servant to pack Clara's belongings into a trunk and to shroud the room in dust sheets.

The same could have been said of his heart. All memories of Clara were packed away neatly, all thoughts of their recent disagreements blanketed with a wilful forgetting. But a heart is not a cold, sparse room, it is a living object and there were moments when his thoughts betrayed him, when the carapace of his heart cracked and let in the light of regret and grief.

On Christmas Eve, a week after her passing, Jacob sat at his desk in the office, Ebenezer in the next room, talking to a client. His partner had left him alone, sensing his mind was elsewhere. Jacob found himself engaging in mental moral arguments, two insistent voices quarrelling in his mind, unwelcome visitors.

Tom Woodburn's death was your doing.

Indeed it was not. He made that voyage of his own choosing. He took the only course available to him in his disgrace: pay off his debts or be sent to debtors' prison.

Yet you had it in your power to reduce those debts, even write them off. Should you not have helped Tom Woodburn more?

No. The careless fire and resulting loss of profit – even the man's death from fever on a ship – only proved how weak and unsuitable he was for Clara. He would have let her down another way, in a hundred other ways.

But what of Clara? He was her chosen one, her beloved. Should you not have helped the man for her sake?

Nonsense. He was not good enough for her. He wasn't half the businessman I am.

All the more reason to help him then. You could have taught him, advised him. What harm could it have done?

It was the principle. It was bad business. I haven't toiled all these years to make flawed decisions. And the hard truth is, it was all for nought, as she was going to die anyway.

This last thought dropped like a stone. Its hardness shocked even Jacob Marley, the crack in his heart splitting further, the warm fluid of feeling leaking out drip by drip. Then crept in a quieter voice, that whispered in his mind's ear.

But if you had helped them ... if she had been with her beloved, giving her strength ... if she had gone with him to warmer climes, to the fresh, mountain air ... might she have survived? Or lived longer, at least? Married him, lived

135

with him, died with him, in happiness? And she would have been happy, with him, away from you, away from your cold grasp …

Jacob stood up from his desk so hurriedly, he knocked over his inkwell that spilled blackly over his work like the spreading mark of death. He stared at it, unable to think what on earth he might do about it, his mind numb, his hands shaking.

'No,' he said aloud. 'This will not do.' The sound of his voice helped to drown out the interior monologue that haunted his thoughts. He marched through to their shrinking clerk Perkins at his desk and barked instructions at him to clean up the mess. He was going home as he was unwell. He passed by his partner's room, whose door was ajar and who glanced at him, his eyes somewhat concerned yet simultaneously trying to focus on this client he was undoubtedly screwing for payment. Jacob nodded to Ebenezer, took his coat and hat and went out without a word into the murky grey of the evening fog.

He stalked home, cold to his bones, regretting the choice not to bring the scarf that Clara had knitted for him last winter. Preparations for the morrow's festivities were in full swing on the streets, in the warmly lit shop windows and warmly lit hearts of the passers-by but he had no eye for it, no heart for it himself. He reached his house, his empty house. He had dismissed the two servants he and Clara had kept just the day before, with no bonus, no references. He had no need of servants now, he could fend for himself, could buy his meals from the tavern on the corner, make a bowl of gruel for his supper if need be. One could live so cheaply on one's own, especially a man, with no female fripperies to fund. He climbed the steps to his front door and went in, closing it behind him with a heavy thud, which resounded dully across the cold tiles of the entrance hall.

He had no stomach for food that night, no hunger for anything but a kind of oblivion from his thoughts. Tomorrow was Christmas Day and there was no mark of it in the rooms, no holly sprig or red ribbon, such as Clara used to tinker with each year at this time. Christmas meant nothing to him, but she had had a fondness for it. He removed his coat and hat and directly went upstairs to a cabinet in the bedroom, in which he kept a bottle of tawny port to take the edge off the cold nights. He rarely drank to excess but always had a nip at bedtime. Instead of his usual small toddy glass he retrieved a wine glass and filled it. He sat on his bed and sipped, the reddened warm liquid slipping down his gullet like blood. He sipped again, hearing a whisper of the voices from earlier and thus took a gulp, wincing at its passage and the resulting fog that webbed his head and made him close his eyes. He suddenly felt immensely tired and had not the vigour to undress, only mustering the effort to slip off his shoes. He placed his glass beside the bed and climbed in beneath the sheets. Sleep would come soon, he told himself, and the voices would stop for a few hours at least. He would go into the office tomorrow, Ebenezer would be there, eschewing the annual invitation to his deceased sister's family Christmas dinner as he always did. *Good friend, Ebenezer*, thought Jacob Marley. Always to be relied upon for a sensible attitude to the poppycock of festivity and family, the foolish lures away from work, the humbug of life.

But sleep did not come. His eyelids were closed, but his eyes were strangely alive behind them, moving this way and that, as if searching for something. He sat up in bed, wide awake, the fog outside casting a peculiar yellow glow across the room. He was aware of an icy draught issuing from the gap underneath his bedroom door. He had forgotten to close his bed curtains. He hopped out of bed, thought about removing his clothes and putting on his nightgown, but it felt too damnably cold for that. So, he drew round the bed curtains, reaching out to take a quick swig of his port before settling back behind them, under the sheets again, pulling the blanket up to his chin, the air about him denser and a little warmer, that blasted draught now shut out. He closed his eyes again, but the draught returned, colder than ever, tickling his nose and nipping his ears.

Perhaps there was a gap in the curtains he had not noticed. He opened his eyes again, resolving to find out. But instead, a curtain twitched. He stared at it, blinked, thought it a trick of the dim, jaundiced dark of the room. But there it was again, a veritable twitch. Then, a small, pale hand appeared, grasping the edge of the curtain. Jacob cried out and recoiled. In the same moment, the hand drew back the curtain and there came such a bright issuing of light that it blinded him. He cried out again and put his hands to his eyes, the light so bright it pained them.

'Jacob,' came a voice, a faint whispering voice as if floating upon the breeze from far away. 'Jacob,' it said again, closer now, warmer and in the room itself.

He opened his fingers a crack to peer out between them, to find the provenance of this strange voice speaking his name. The light was still as bright as summer sunshine, but amidst it he saw a shape, the form of a person, a female person, with long, fair hair and the face of … the face of … could it be? There stood his sister, his beloved Clara Belle. The light was fading now and he could discern her more clearly. Her cheeks were rounded and pink, her hair a golden cloud about her face, threaded festively with the leaves and berries of holly and mistletoe. She wore a cloak of green, of red, of silver and black, dotted with stars that twinkled merrily. She was smiling at him, her eyes laughing, her lips rosy. She looked the very picture of health and happiness, so bonny it made his heart sing.

'Oh, my life! Oh, my dear sister!'

'Jake, my dear brother,' she said, as she used to call his boyhood self. Her voice flowed with infinite kindness, her smile a balm to his grieving heart.

But as he gazed at her in wonder, he saw curious qualities about her that were not so healthful and not like her image in life. Her face around her red cheeks shone with an unnatural pallor and emanated specks of whiteness that floated about her head as if on a warm draught, as if she had been dusted with flour in a bakery. Her hair, though luscious and yellow, he now saw was scored through with metallic silver and dark stripes of lead-grey. Most oddly, her eyes were not the cornflower blue she had in life but instead were black, pure black, blacker than any night sky and deeper than any well. To stare into them was to lose oneself, to fall headlong into a never-ending abyss; they drew him in yet terrified him, so that he had to turn away.

'You cannot look upon me,' she said, her voice more like her own now, but curiously choral, as if several Claras spoke at once, some higher, some lower. He forced his eyes upwards and saw those black wells again, turned upon him now and topped with a frown. She spoke again. 'This is no courtesy call, Jacob. This is a visitation. I come with words of warning. Ignore them at your peril.'

Despite the undoubted joy he experienced at the presence of his sister again, Jacob felt an icy fear run through his veins at her words. His instinct was to fling the curtain back across her and hide beneath the bedclothes. Either that, or leap from his bed and run, run down the stairs and out into the street, away from the terrible and wonderful, awful and beautiful being beside him.

She said no more, only glaring at him. His voice, small and meek beside her own choir, spoke up: 'Speak them then, sister, for it seems I must hear them.'

But she did not speak, instead holding out her pale, little hand to his. He was loathe to take it, but she moved it closer still, outstretched, gleaming white. He put his hand in hers and in an instant, the bed curtains were gone, the bed vanished, the walls and ceiling dissolved and the solid old house itself fell away and his feet had left the earth.

Holding fast onto his sister's hand, he felt them shoot upwards at an alarming rate, then stop and hover in the air. He dared not look down, instead closing his eyes tight shut and calling out to her to stop it and bring them back to earth, which she ignored coolly. They moved forwards and the rush of movement whistled in his ears, but he was neither cold nor shivering; there was a curious stasis about his body that meant he felt the same as he had on the ground. Eventually, curiosity got the better of him and he opened his eyes. They were gliding over London, the rooftops and chimneys and spires scrolling beneath them. Then they came to a stop and began to descend, down, down into a dark alleyway in one of the shabbiest parts of the city, an alleyway he recognised, and a body lying prone in it that he recognised, and the gurgling sound of a man whose throat had been cut and was breathing his last that he recognised too. It was the well-to-do man whose purse he had taken all those decades ago. He watched the man die, hovering above him beside his sister, whose face was implacable.

Then, she spoke, her words coming to him like an old knowledge, like a voice inside his own head, 'You did not call for help.'

'No, I did not. Look, see, he was going to die anyway.'

'The money he was carrying, half of which you stole.'

'Yes, he was fat and rich and had no need of it, since he were about to die.'

'It was meant for others. His children. They were in need.'

Clara put an arm lightly about his shoulders and in an instant, they were in another place, in a drawing room of a fine house. There were three children there, seated on a chaise longue, holding onto each other, weeping inconsolably. Before them was a policeman and a maid. Jacob could not hear their words, but the situation looked grave.

'These were his children. Their mother was dead and the father was in debt. He had won the money at the gaming tables and was taking it to pay off some debts. When he died, the children were left with nothing and were sent to a school for orphans, where they were beaten and mistreated. Two died there of disease and another became a cruel person, who beat his wife and children, as he had learned nothing more at school.'

Jacob stared at the crying children and recalled Clara and himself in a similar position, after the death of their parents.

'It is not my fault.'

'What is not?'

'What happened to that man's children.'

'I do not speak of fault. I am merely showing you the facts.'

And with that, they whisked off again, across the streets and alleyways to alight in east London, at a row of cramped and filthy houses, a river of sewage in the middle of the roadway, a filthy rag pegged on a line here, an empty cage of a long-dead songbird hanging there. The roof of a nearby house seemed to shimmer then vanish, and they were able to see the inhabitants, as if it were a great doll's house.

'Here is Mrs Lila Ketteridge,' said Clara. 'And that is her blind husband, Dick. See how they sit beside a fireplace with no fire in it. They recall the feeling of warmth on their feet, but they have no money to buy fuel. See, they have already burnt all of the doors and window frames. There are no children there. The last one died of hunger after we called in their final loan. Dick will be dead soon of fever and Lila will throw herself in the river.'

'I see what this is,' said Jacob. 'You are trying to blame me for their situation.'

'I am not judging you, Jacob. Only showing you the consequences of our actions. Let us see more.'

They ranged on over London and visited the home of Mrs Gilvin who had gout and six children, now only two children left, her left foot so swollen she lived in her bed and was fed gruel by her eldest, a sweep with a terrible cough. They did not visit the homes of Mrs Bainbridge and Mrs Lee, instead sweeping on to a desolate, crowded graveyard, where neither had tombstones to remember them by, as both were buried in paupers' graves, some short months after their loans were called in by Jacob.

'What do you say to this, Jacob?'

'I say, this was business. It was them or us. Our survival was guaranteed by their situation. We did not cause them to need to borrow money. And we helped them by giving them the money they needed. All they had to do was pay it back. We could not afford to be charitable. Not with the Mrs Clayburns of this world, ready to snatch a purse from children.'

'I have shown you some scenes from your past,' Clara's choral voice came in his ear. 'All dead and gone, the past. But the present is with us and there are more of your clients to behold.'

Next, Clara took him over the homes of some of the poorest of his current clients. Some were out working on Christmas Eve till late, trudging home weary and hungry; some were preparing paltry gifts for their children or plucking a skinny bird to cook for ten mouths; others were young and hungry, lying in bed dreaming of the morrow, their legs twisting with pain at the rickets or clutching their stomachs with other maladies, the shadows under their parents' eyes showing their powerless concern.

Clara said, 'You have the wherewithal to be more generous now, Jacob. You are not fighting for survival on the streets now. Where is your mercy? Where is your charity?'

'If I were to show it, we would not last long in the business. Our expenditure would outweigh our profit and from that only misery is derived. Everyone who is not with us is against us and if they owe us something, I will ensure we receive it, to the last. Everyone gets their just desserts.'

Clara pinched the back of his neck hard, so hard he cried out and looked at her. Those black eyes sucked him in and he could not look away, as much as they terrified him.

'And what of Uncle Robert?'

In a moment, they were above a tall, Georgian house in a smart part of town. In a large, four-poster bed lay an old man, covered in blankets edged with brocade, snoring with great abandon.

'He's doing very nicely,' said Clara. 'But you vowed

revenge on him, Jacob. Why did you not seek it, when you had the means? He has not had his just desserts.'

Jacob glared at the man in the bed and felt a sour taste in his mouth. Oh, how he had dreamt of avenging their childhood misery upon this selfish man. But Robert Marley had become a leading figure at the stock exchange. Once Scrooge & Marley was up and running, there was no question of attacking in any way this bastion of the business. It would have been professional suicide.

'It was bad business. I cannot have a vendetta against such a man. It is too late now and too long ago. Anyway, he is old now and will probably die soon. He will die alone. I pity him somewhat.'

'So you have pity for a man who wronged you so cruelly yet no pity for those who have done nothing to you except fail to meet your strict terms of money-lending?'

'I keep telling you, it is business. Nothing will ever change that cold, hard fact.'

Again, the sharp pinch on the back of the neck and Clara said in a low voice that resounded with bitterness, 'Let me show you another cold, hard fact. What saltwater and sealife does to a soft, human body.'

They lifted up high into the sky, so high it took Jacob's breath away and he choked, gasping for breath. They whizzed on over London to the mighty, dirty Thames wending its way through the dirty old town, fringed by foraging mudlarks and corpses of dogs and citizens. They followed its course out to sea. For many miles they rounded the coast of England, so far and so long that Jacob felt he would expire from exhaustion but at last they began to slow, over a stretch of ocean that was lightened by the coming sun. They descended, gathering speed until the surface of the sea came at them like a locomotive and Jacob screamed in terror, lest they should be smashed to pieces by the rolling waves. But in they plunged and yet the air still breathed in his lungs, his eyes still focused clearly, the sea below the surface azure and clear, shot through with sun rays from above, populated by exotic sealife of many colours, a narrow-eyed turtle and, off in the bluish distance, the dark shapes of big fish circling. They approached a figure on the seabed, its rotting white body providing a sumptuous feast for many a glassy-eyed fish, nibbling at its flesh, its soft parts, its toes, its knees, its innards, its neck and there on its face, its eye sockets were hollow but Jacob recoiled as he still knew that face, he knew whose body this was, abandoned at the bottom of the ocean. It was Tom Woodburn.

Jacob tried to close his eyes but there was that pinch again – harder than ever – and he turned to look at his sister, her eyes now so wide and black that they seemed to take over her face that brimmed with darkness and made him gape his mouth with wondrous fear and pity.

Another tap on his shoulder and the sea collapsed beneath them, like water thrown on fresh paint it simply slid away and darkness fell on them like a shroud. They were back standing beside his bed, but it was daylight and in his bed was a figure. It was himself, an older man, white-haired and dead. Yes, dead, the final moment having just left him, his face sinking slightly, settling into its eternal death mask. Then, from the body issued a curious wisp, a stringy spiral of cloud-like whiteness that coalesced into a shape; that of himself, in his day clothes, his pigtail, his tights and boots. His spirit floated serenely upwards, but then other forms began to appear: firstly, around his waist a clinking sound announced the arrival of links in a chain. The chain formed around his waist and floated down from his body quite some way, along its length forming other objects all wrought in gleaming metal, the tools of his trade, such as cash-boxes and purses, padlocks and their keys and a variety of documents that scrolled and unscrolled as they formed.

His spiritual self was trussed tightly by these accoutrements, still in a ghostly sleep, unaware of its nature bound by these heavy, clanking burdens. The body began to turn slowly, the feet falling and the head rising, the objects resounding horribly as they fell against each other and weighted his spirit down a notch, which then rose with a great effort that made its eyes spring open. Jacob watched in horror as his spectral self awoke, looked down upon itself and saw the fact of its eternity; it began to open its great mouth, that fell open too far and too low for human possibility, so that his shrieking mouth was twice the length of his head and the desperate scream that issued from it rang in Jacob's earthly ears so jangling and loud it drove his senses mad with horror.

'Oh, woe is me!' cried Jacob, flinging his hands before his eyes to escape the scene.

His sister's voice came, a mighty chorus now of a thousand Claras, shrill and epic in his ears: 'See your fate, Jacob Marley. These chains are those you have forged yourself, an extra link added with each selfish act. This is not your business, mark me. Humanity is your business. Hear me, my brother, or pay this price for eternity!'

'I cannot bear it! It cannot be true!'

Instantly, he felt himself fall and then a cracking thump, as he landed on a bed, his own bed, his own curtains around him. He looked about him and saw that it was daylight. He flung open the bed curtain to look for his sister, but she was nowhere to be seen. He jumped off his bed and stumbled to the window and saw that the fog had lifted, that it was frosty and clear, that people scurried to and fro on Christmas morning, hailing passers-by with festive cheer, all accompanied by the sound of many bells ringing out the day across the city.

Jacob looked around his room and rubbed his eyes. It truly was morning, he truly was here, in his room, on Christmas Day. Gone were the dark streets of London, the miserable clients, Uncle Robert, Tom's corpse and his sister's spirit, beautiful and terrible all at once, all gone. Dazed, he stood and considered it all, ran it over like a series of flickering photographs in his mind, so solid they seemed, so real. But it was morning and these things had happened in his bed, at night. A dream. Surely, a dream, indubitably, a dream.

'Humbug,' said Jacob Marley.

He realised he was still in his dishevelled clothes from yesterday, so resolved to wash and change. In the midst of scrubbing his neck, he stopped and winced from pain. He had only one mirror, for shaving, and so could not look to see the cause of the discomfort on the back of his neck. He touched it gingerly and felt a ridged lump there, sorely tender, as if a stork had that very night picked him up and pinched harshly on his tender neck with its sharp beak. Then, with a chill, he remembered Clara, her ghostly hand cold and bony on his neck, pinching him three times, the last the worst, at the sight of her beloved Tom's corpse at the bottom of the sea. A shiver ran up his spine and ended with a shudder at the source of the pain on his neck. He stopped and thought for a moment.

'Humbug,' he said again.

He walked quickly to his counting-house that day, resolutely ignoring the celebratory atmosphere surrounding him. He found Scrooge already at work, a wry look of disdain writ on his face at his partner's unusually late arrival.

'I cannot think you were making merry last night, Jacob,' he said. 'That would be most unlike you.'

Jacob stopped and stared at his friend, the images of the previous night parading through his mind's eye like the memory of a horrible theatrical entertainment.

'Ebenezer, do you believe …'

He stopped and gulped down a bitter bile that rose up his throat.

'Believe what?' snapped Scrooge, his expression curious but about to turn to derision.

'That … spirits …' Jacob said, his hand absently

152

reaching for the sore patch on the back of his neck. 'That spirits walk the earth?'

'I do not!' scoffed Scrooge. 'Have you been at the port, man?'

Jacob's hand fell and he looked down at his boots. He had a vision of his life passing this way, his eyes turned down, away from those around him, away from the misery of the city, safe only here, here in his counting-house with his friend, Scrooge, and his ledgers and bills and letters and money.

'Yes,' he said. 'Yes, that's it. I had a little port. My senses must have been disturbed by it. That is all. That is all.'

Scrooge was already back at his work before the end of his partner's utterance, which drove Marley to pull himself up by his boot-straps and go to his desk, whereupon he took up his pen and ink and fell to writing great long lists of figures and felt much comforted.

Epilogue

Clara watched over her brother Jacob, seated at his desk, his pen scratching out lines of numbers in perfectly neat script. She shook her head with pity.

She thought, *I could not have done more. He is wilfully blind when he wants to be, belligerently ignorant when he chooses. There is nothing more I could show him that might change his mind. But there is time. There are many years before Death will come for him. Perhaps my visitation will weigh upon his mind and he will awake one morning and change his ways. Yet I can do no more. I have done my duty by him. As my beloved Tom once wrote to me, I will leave this earth with no incomplete business. It is as true for me now as it was for him then. And now I can go to him, in the dwelling-place of light, where he waits for me.*

She looked about her at this abode of waiting, this shining sky of souls who drift down to earth to finish their affairs, weighed down with regrets and anxieties for those they left behind. Her soul felt weightless, not empty or hollow, but free as the air, a being forged from radiance.

She drifted upwards, the world and all its cares falling away from her. As she rose, she thought she saw sparkles of white about her, then felt the wintry surprise of snowflakes falling on her face and her upturned hands. Before her, within the luminosity she sought, the faint outlines of shapes were forming. There was a house, a tall white house on a smart, clean street. Outside it stood a horse and trap, the animal familiar to her, which snuffled, then stamped its feet in the gathering drifts. Beside the horse, waiting patiently on the pavement, sat a dog, a mish-mash of colours and a fluffy tail that wagged lazily and thumped on the cold ground, sending up white, frozen puffs of snow. She floated past them into the house, along the hallway hung with garlands, the scent of pine sharp about them, the red berries of holly and white berries of mistletoe studding the green swathes like jolly polka-dots. She entered a room, hung with pale blue curtains with silver tassels, the damask upholstery of the suite matching this blue perfectly, the blue of her mother's eyes. On a table was laid a tureen of punch, beside silver dishes of chestnuts and almonds, surrounding a great plate upon which rested a sumptuous turkey and roasted vegetables, its bronzed skin glistening in the dancing light of the roaring fire in the grate. A blackly fruited pudding sat behind it, blue with flickering flames.

Alongside the table stood three figures, all gazing upon her and smiling. First, her father – oh, dear chap! – in his favourite top hat. Then, her mother – oh, Mama! – those blue eyes shining with love. Last, stood her intended, young and strong, his hand outstretched to welcome her – oh, my darling! – her Tom.

She felt his stubby fingers entwine with hers, his big arms encircle her and his soft lips meet her own. As she turned to greet her family, she breathed in the air of her eternity. It was rich with the spiced and woodland scents of Christmas, past, present and yet to come.

Afterword

by Rebecca Mascull

I met Vanessa Lafaye through words before I met her in person. We read each other's first novels at the same time and were soon in contact via Twitter, genuinely delighted to find another writer who seemed to share the same preoccupations about history and delight in the same love of language. We also soon discovered a mutual passion for Dickens. We were part of the marvellous author's collective, The Prime Writers, together. For the next few years, we talked on Skype and on the phone and messaged and met up when we could, despite living at other ends of the country. She was smart, funny, wise and caring. She'd talk to me for hours about writing, love and life. She listened and advised. She talked and shared her thoughts. She helped me through some tough times. She was a wonderful friend. The whole time I knew her, she had cancer. It did not define her.

She was too full of the wonder of the world to allow that to be so. Not long before she died, she was on a trip of a lifetime around New Zealand. She was messaging me from a ship, writing this book. We were discussing Scrooge's timeline, his apprenticeship, his sister and so forth. I photographed some pages from *A Christmas Carol* and messaged them to her. We had a great chat about Dickens, as we often did. A short while later, we messaged about the book again. She said she would finish it soon. She said she wanted to talk with me about her next project. We arranged to talk the following week. She died three days later. I never got to have that talk.

When I wrote to her husband, I had no idea what to say. I thought I'd scroll through our old messages to see what we talked about when we first met. The scrolling got stuck and wouldn't load any more. It had stopped at a years old message from V (I always called her V) that said simply, 'We should start *A Christmas Carol* appreciation society!' I had no memory of that conversation. Not long after, V's editor from HarperCollins – Kate Mills – got in touch with me and asked me if I would like to finish writing *Miss Marley*. Of course, I said yes. It felt absolutely right. Our similar writing styles; our mutual adoration of Mr Dickens (I've recalled since that I mention him in two of my novels!); our discussions while she was writing the book and the fact that I collect copies of *A Christmas Carol* and I am somewhat obsessed with it, all made me feel that it was the right thing to do. I found out I had the blessings of her husband and her other close writer friends. The message about our appreciation society seemed to be a message for me to accept the challenge.

I read through the nine chapters she had already written. I loved her story, her characterisation, her use of choice Victorian details and beautiful language. I printed it out and covered it in notes, annotating for the elements of her style and imagery, her character motifs and plot points. I had a growing sense of where I felt the story should go. At my first meeting with Kate, we looked through V's notes and realised there was very little on the ending. I discussed it with other writer friends and we all came to the conclusion that there was no conclusion as such. So, I had to go with my gut and write the ending I felt flowed naturally from the work she had already produced. I drew on our friendship and knowledge of her previous writing, but I didn't overthink it. I let it pour out, as I'd heard V herself had done when she was writing those early chapters against the clock. I wrote Chapter Ten to the end in five days. It was like an act of channelling. It was exhausting and beautiful. Sometimes I felt as if she were very close by. I will never forget it. I will always be grateful. I hope I did a good job, V.

Rebecca Mascull, June 2018

Rebecca Mascull is the author of three historical novels and also writes saga novels as Mollie Walton. She has previously worked in education, has a Masters in Writing and lives by the sea in the east of England.

ONE PLACE. MANY STORIES

Bold, innovative and
empowering publishing.

FOLLOW US ON:

@HQStories